MOST WONDERFUL TIME

TONI SHILOH

Copyright © 2021 by Toni Shiloh.

All rights reserved. No part of this book may be reproduced, stored in a retrieval system, or transmitted in any form or by any means—electronic, mechanical, photocopying, recording, scanning or other—for brief quotations embodied in critical reviews or articles, without the prior written permission of the publisher and certain other noncommercial uses permitted by copyright law.

Scripture taken from the New King James Version®. Copyright © 1982 by Thomas Nelson. Used by permission. All rights reserved.

Cover design by Toni Shiloh.

Cover art photos © Depositphotos.com/Milkos (Kostiantyn Postumitenko) and arquiplay77 (Pablo Scapinachis Armstrong) used by permission.

Published in the United States of America by Toni Shiloh.

www.ToniShiloh.com

Most Wonderful Time is a work of fiction. Names, characters, places, and incidents are either products of the author's imagination or used fictitiously. All characters are fictional, and any similarity to people living or dead is purely coincidental.

❀ Created with Vellum

Dedication

To the Author and Finisher of my faith.

Chapter One

With coffee in hand and snow falling from the sky, Gabe Lewis could really believe the lyrics that crooned over the bank lobby's speakers of this being the most wonderful time of the year. The Christmas season always brought out the best in his family. Dad would act more sociable. Mom would start baking like crazy and dropping off cookies just because. Not to mention, he'd see his brothers and sisters more.

Though the calendar hadn't flipped to December yet, Thanksgiving had come and gone so people were in full holiday swing and ready to count down to Christmas. He grinned as Pentatonix continued to sing acapella about the *most wonderful time* while he navigated through the still mostly quiet bank. Cornwall & Lewis wouldn't open for another half hour, and the early morning stillness was the best part of the day.

Lord, thank You for another day. May You bless the people who walk through these doors. Help us give the best customer service and meet our customers' needs. Please provide for those who come through here, even if we can't.

He whispered an "amen," then began his route through the building. He started by dropping a to-go coffee cup at Lorlaine's desk—the mortgage manager's executive assistant—and continued down the hall. He headed for one of the loan officer's desks and dropped off another cup, though the sugared slush Beth drank shouldn't be called coffee. Two more drinks remained, one for him and the other for Dad.

First, he needed to lose his parka and grab the files for the end-of-year meeting. Dad had probably been in the office for a couple of hours already. The man lived and breathed all things banking, while Gabe simply liked numbers. He was good at calculations and spreadsheets didn't make him shudder. Following in Dad's footsteps after high school had seemed like the smartest choice.

Only now that he was about to turn thirty-one, his view on time —and how little of it he had left to do something amazing—shifted. He'd always figured hitting thirty would somehow bring him a family, resembling his sisters' lives. Well, not Eve so much as Angel and Starr. They were happy, married, and living a life he wanted. Angel recently became a stepmom to a pistol of a little girl, while Waylon and Starr were coming up on two years of marriage.

Both sisters were enjoying life to the fullest.

He'd be lying if he didn't admit to being a tad envious. Gabe thought the thirties would have him married, but he still hadn't found the right woman. As clichéd as the expression sounded, it remained true. He dated, put himself out there, but so far no one made him want to get down on one knee and commit to forever. His older brother Noel teased him about being commitment shy, but that wasn't true. Simply put, Gabe's wishes hadn't lined up with timing.

Despite his singleness, he'd woken in a good mood this morning. Not annoyingly so but with a little pep to his step. Granted it could have been the mug of coffee he'd consumed at home or the one he'd drink in Dad's office. Regardless, he liked to think that God was smiling on him and something special would happen today. Gabe just didn't know what yet.

He maneuvered the tray of coffees into one hand, tucking his folder under his arm to free up a hand to knock on his father's door.

"Enter."

Gabe twisted the knob then shut the door quietly behind him before turning to greet Dad. "Morning." He halted. A beautiful woman sat in the chair Gabe usually occupied. Although her hair had been pulled back into a severe bun and glasses took up most of her face, her beauty couldn't be hidden.

And he'd only brought two coffees.

"Ah, just on time, Gabriel. Meet Shanée Mitchell. Ms. Mitchell, this is my son and our operations manager, Gabriel Lewis."

Gabe handed a coffee cup to his dad then turned to the woman. "Please, call me Gabe." He offered a hand. "Nice to meet you."

Her lips thinned into a tight smile. Her handshake was firm and a little on the brusque side. Had he upset her? Interrupted an important conversation?

"Was this a private meeting? I forgot to check the calendar for any changes before coming in."

"No, not at all, son. Have a seat." Dad leaned back in his chair, his suit coat gaping with the movement.

Gabe sat in the vacant chair, wondering why his tie suddenly felt too tight. He peered at the new employee. "Sorry, I would have gotten a coffee order for you if I'd known." He spoke kind of out the side of his mouth. Not that he was shy or trying to avoid looking directly in her face but . . .

Yeah, he totally was. Something about her intimidated him. But he couldn't figure out what. Was it the *back off* sign across her forehead? The fake smile she offered when they shook hands? The way she'd tried to squeeze his fingers as if daring him to crush hers too tightly, or worse, give one of those flimsy handshakes?

"I don't drink coffee."

Or maybe it was the no-nonsense way she spoke. Like she didn't want to be in this office, Cornwall & Lewis, or even in the District of Columbia. Worse, maybe she hated Christmas, and the awesome music running through the speakers had brought out the Scrooge in her.

But none of that would stop him from being friendly. "The café sells tea as well."

Her lips pursed.

Okay, not a tea drinker either. Gabe met his dad's gaze, waiting for him to explain what was going on.

"We're putting our end-of-the-year meeting off until tomorrow."

Gabe nodded.

"Instead, I'm hoping you'll show Ms. Mitchell around. She'll be our new internal auditor."

Joy. Gabe forced a smile as he looked at her, only she had her hand clasped over her knee, her focus on one of the men named in Cornwall & Lewis. *Of course. Pay attention to the boss, not the underling.*

Gabe shook his head. Since when did he put himself down like that? He usually had more self-confidence. One meeting with the new internal auditor—who he'd had no clue they were getting— and he reverted to his teenage years of internal snark and self-deprecation.

"I'm assuming Noel already knows."

"Yes. He's already met Ms. Mitchell."

Of course. Noel and Dad were always at the office. Gabe wouldn't be surprised if they had a hidden pallet. He settled for false cheer. "Fantastic. Do you want me to simply introduce her to everyone?" *Please let that be all.*

"Oh no." Dad shook his head. "She needs access to all the files and to be shown how everything is done. She'll be taking the office next to yours. It should have been cleaned out over the weekend."

Right. If his father saw a need, he'd make sure it was handled before business hours. The man never slept, at least not that Gabe ever saw.

"I can do that." Because he had no choice.

"Thank you, Gabriel."

Gabe nodded and stood, grabbing his lukewarm coffee and the meeting files that would apparently wait until tomorrow.

Ms. Mitchell reached the closed door before him and opened it.

"Thank you."

"You looked like you had your hands full."

He pointed down the hall with his coffee cup. "We're down here." He spared a glance at the woman, trying to determine her age.

The black bun settled at the nape of her neck actually lent a stylish look instead of making her appear like the proverbial old maid. It just seemed too tight. Didn't that hurt? Her black suit conformed to her figure and looked more comfortable. However, she wore the flattest, *ugliest* looking shoes he'd ever seen. His sisters always walked in stilts. Granted, they were all under five-five, with Eve being the tallest.

Actually, Ms. Mitchell seemed around Eve's height. Yet all the cataloguing didn't lend a single clue as to what kind of person she was.

He cleared his throat. "How long have you been an internal auditor?"

"Since your dad hired me."

Okay. "What did you do before that?"

Her eyes flashed at him. "I was in the Air Force."

Gabe almost forgot the *back off* sign. *Almost.* Personal questions were definitely off limits with this one. He took a deep breath to search for some holiday spirit despite the frost coming his way and stopped in front of her office. *Lord, I could use some help.*

"After you," he gestured.

Shanée wanted to slam the door in the face of the smiling man and work in solitude. Fortunately the past ten years with the Air Force had taught her how to cooperate with the most difficult people in the name of teamwork. Especially when the assignment wasn't one she'd asked for or expected.

Relocating to Washington D.C. hadn't been in her plans. She'd intended to be a lifer—retire after twenty-plus years serving her country. But one freak incident skiing with her squadron left her back messed up enough for the military to decide to medically retire her after ten years of service. Now she collected a disability paycheck every month, saw a physical therapist way too often, and was forced to wear these horrid shoes until her back decided to quit spasming over the slightest thing. If she wore the cute little high heels that remained in her closet, she'd be in a world of hurt.

She eyed the chair behind the desk and sighed. At least Mr. Lewis had remembered the ergonomic chair requirement. Hopefully she wouldn't have to grab the extra back cushion she had stashed in her vehicle.

"So, Lewis—"

"Gabe," the cheerful man interjected.

Why couldn't she just call him by his last name and call it a day? And why was he still beaming? He was probably one of those morning people. The maniac edge of his smile reminded her of Buddy the Elf. *Ugh.*

Shanée pulled in a deep breath, but not one so deep it would make her back twinge. "Gabe."

His grin widened, showing a row of pearly whites. Wow, she'd found out the real reason Mr. Lewis was a banker. He probably paid a pretty penny to get his son's teeth so perfect. Gabe Lewis could be a model in a toothpaste commercial. *Focus, Mitchell.*

"Gabe, if you would please give me a rundown of the system here, I'm sure I can figure everything else out." *Then leave. Stat!*

"Oh, Gabe," a woman called out in the hall, passing by. "Thanks for the coffee." She held up a to-go container in salute.

"My pleasure, Lorlaine."

"I'll get yours tomorrow," she said as she walked out of view.

"And steal my thunder?" Gabe countered, sticking his head out the door.

Lewis—*Gabe*—shook his head as if he couldn't believe someone wanted to buy their own coffee. Did he do this all year or were his actions specific to spreading holiday cheer? Had it been rude of her to decline a cup? Unfortunately, her life needed to be caffeine free now. The nerve pain medications she took didn't interact well when she drank caffeine, which meant she'd stopped drinking her morning coffee and indulging in her afternoon Frappuccinos. Life now really was dark.

Shanée knew she should have stuck to the belief that Black people didn't ski, but no, the squadron commander had assured everyone that the fun day skiing event would be that—*fun*. How wrong he'd been. When her skis had slid from underneath her and she'd continued her journey down the not-so-bunny slope, the tree in her path had her trying to roll out of the way. Only her ski caught on a rock and she'd flipped around, hitting her back against the oak.

A surgery later, then a med board with goodbyes from her fellow Airmen, had Shanée creating plan B for her life. Which was how she'd ended up with a job as an internal auditor at Cornwall & Lewis. Stuck in a small eight-by-ten office with Buddy the Elf.

"How many cups of coffee did you buy?" she asked.

"Only four, and one was mine and the other was for Dad." He shrugged his shoulders. "Some people are still on vacation from Thanksgiving so it's a little quiet around the office."

"Does that mean if they weren't you would have bought them coffee too?" She tried not to study him like a specimen under a microscope, but really.

"Well, Rick doesn't drink coffee but always asks for Earl Grey. Claire prefers tea as well. My brother Noel has a coffee maker in his office, so I don't bother ordering anything for him."

Her eyebrows rose. "How many siblings do you have?" Not that she cared, but just how deep did Mr. Lewis's nepotism run? Did they all work here?

"That work here? Just the one. Noel is one of our loan officers."

"And the others?" Did he ever say how many there were?

"My sisters don't work here."

She nodded in understanding.

Gabe clapped his hands. "One of our IT guys will set you up with an account. Once they do that, you'll have access to the system." He pointed to the desk phone. "Jeff's number is on speed dial. Simply introduce yourself and he'll get you situated. Once that happens, I can walk you through the system."

Shanée hated meeting new people, but the Air Force had taught her to do that as well. Still, that didn't prevent the nausea from swirling in her stomach at the thought of introducing herself to some guy she'd never met. "Fine."

"I'm right next door to your right if you need anything before he gets to you."

Shanée nodded but her insides were clapping with glee that Gabe was finally leaving. As he walked away, she slowly sank into her chair and closed her eyes. The chair was perfect. The strain from standing and making idle chitchat vanished.

Before she could change her mind, she picked up the phone and pressed the button labeled *Jeff in IT*.

"This is Jeff, how can I help you today?"

Drat. Another cheerful person. Then again, maybe Cornwall & Lewis would turn out to be a good company to work for if all these people were so happy. "Hi, I'm the new internal auditor and I need to get an account set up so I can have computer access."

"You must be Shanée Mitchell." He pronounced it Shaw-nee.

She winced. "It's *Shaw-ney*."

"I'm sorry, Shanée. I have you scheduled for a ten a.m. setup. I can't get to your office until then. Will that do?"

Did she have any other choice? She bit back a sigh. Lately her options were ripped away at every fork in the road, leaving her on a trail with too many curves and no way to get off. "Yes. Thank you."

"My pleasure."

She eyed the clock hanging above the wall. Would they let her decorate her office? If so, that plain black and white rectangular clock would be gone by the end of the day. It was too sterile. And apparently only nine o'clock. She had an hour to spare. She turned her gaze to the wall separating her from Gabe Lewis. Did she dare ask him for a task until Jeff could give her an account?

No. He was too inquisitive, and she didn't want to share

anything with him. She just wanted to *be*, figure out a way to cope with life, and hope that the new year would be kinder to her.

With a sigh, Shanée rose gingerly to her feet and made her way to Gabe's office. She drew in steady breaths, hoping they would be enough to shore her up against the onslaught that was a happy coworker.

Chapter Two

When his father had instructed Gabe to assist Shanée, he hadn't anticipated seeing her more than once throughout the day. Yet here they were on Friday, scheduling yet another time to go over the inner workings of Cornwall & Lewis. Gabe wanted to complain and ask Dad if Noel could do it, but he already knew the answer.

Noel was being groomed to take over Dad's position after he retired—*if* that ever happened. Most likely he would die one day, and Noel would step in next. A morbid thought but one that would probably have Dad grinning and saying "yesss" in that way he did when something went according to his plan.

Somehow, some way, Gabe had convinced Shanée to let their next meeting be a working lunch. She even caved and let him order from the Florida Avenue Grill. The restaurant served the best soul food in D.C. in his opinion. He'd ordered the fried catfish and had been surprised when Shanée asked for smothered pork chops.

Now he was even more curious about where she called home. So far she'd been closed-mouthed about anything relating to her past. Nothing he'd said, no amount of friendliness, had pried the lid open. He'd almost given up trying. After all, no one said you had to become friends with all your coworkers, even if he usually was. But God had been nudging him to keep trying.

Maybe this lunch would do the trick. He set the takeout bags down on the conference table and grabbed some napkins and plastic utensils from the sideboard. He'd already brought in his work laptop and figured Shanée would arrive with hers.

And there she was, fifteen minutes early. He couldn't help but notice how she arrived early to every single meeting, whether in-person or virtual.

"Hey there." He smiled, the act faltering slightly when her lips pursed. He got the feeling she wasn't a smiling type of person, but he literally didn't know what else to do to appear more friendly. Widen his eyes? No, that would probably have her calling HR.

"Hello. Something smells good." She set her laptop and notebook down onto the table.

"You arrived just in time. I've got your pork chops and sides here." He passed her the white container. "Oh, and your drink." He handed her the lemonade she'd requested.

"Thank you. How much was it?"

He paused from opening his own food, then swallowed. "I've got it. Consider it a welcome to the office, plus I never got you that coffee."

"I don't drink coffee, remember?"

He hadn't meant literally. Gabe studied her. Something about her comment rang false. Though he'd never seen her drink a cup, surely she had before. "Never ever?"

She sighed, then slowly looked at him. "Once upon a time."

"What, it too hot or too cold?"

Her lips quirked and he wanted to clap his hands. *Yes!* He knew she had a sense of humor somewhere, even though she was more armored than Ft. Knox. Wait, was that a real thing or just hyperbole?

"You're never going to stop asking questions, are you?"

Gabe kept his face impassive or tried to anyway. "I'm just trying to get to know you."

Her lips twisted. "Despite the fact that it's very obvious I don't want to share my personal life with people at work? That I just want to do my job?"

Gabe bit back a sigh at the sound of frustration in her voice. "I'm sorry, Shanée. I wasn't trying to make you feel uncomfortable. I just had the feeling you needed a friend." Saying God told him to make friends with her was a little weird considering they knew nothing about one another.

Clearly, she'd already marked him in the *annoying and strange* column already.

Her gaze shifted away, and if he wasn't mistaken, her bottom lip trembled. "Maybe I do need a friend," she whispered.

"I'm a good listener. At least, my mom and sisters are always telling me so."

She snorted. "How many sisters *do* you have?"

"If I answer, then you have to tell me why no caffeine."

"Fine." She blew out a breath. "I had an accident in the military. I'm on medication for the aftereffects, and no, it doesn't affect my work performance."

He held up his hands. "I wasn't judging or even thinking that."

She nodded slowly. "Anyway, I'm one of those people who have the lovely benefit of not being able to have caffeine while on the medication. It gave me nasty side effects so I'm going without now."

"Do you miss it?"

"So much," she sighed. "Do you know how hard it is to wake up in the morning without that glorious first cup? Then I come in to work and you're all chipper, flaunting your drink in my face." Her dark brown eyes met his. "I hate it."

He laughed. He hadn't meant to, couldn't have stopped the chuckle if he'd tried. The emotion bubbled up and out, and he leaned over his catfish, trying to gasp for air. "I knew you hated me, but who knew it was because of the coffee?"

Shanée cracked a smile. "I have a list. It's not *just* the coffee."

"Ouch." He rubbed his chest. "Maybe I'll prove those things wrong."

"Not as long as you keep coming in so cheerful and waving dark roast in the air."

He sighed. "I did bring you a lemonade today. Doesn't that fix it?"

She took a long sip of the beverage. "It's a step in the right direction."

Gabe smiled, said grace, then took a bite of his food. Now that the tension had been broken, he felt lighter. "I have three sisters. Eve is the oldest. She's right after Noel."

"Aww, so you're the middle child?"

"Well, I'm actually a twin. Angel and I are third in birth order, and Starr is the youngest."

"Five of you, huh?" That was a lot of kids. "Your mother must be a saint."

"You know it."

Shanée laughed, and Gabe responded with a grin. He'd made her laugh now, maybe they would be okay and be able to have a friendly relationship at work.

Their conversation shifted to work and as they ate, Shanée continued the line of questions she'd started yesterday. The inner workings of a bank made Gabe's eyes want to cross, but he knew every answer. Maybe that's why Dad had tasked him with this assignment, as tedious as he found it.

"Earth to Gabe."

His head jerked up. "Sorry. My brain found a rabbit trail."

"Well, dangle a carrot back my way."

He chuckled. "Right. Sorry. Repeat whatever it was you said."

Shanée's gaze roamed his face. "You're not into this, are you?"

"Into what?"

She lifted her hand, gesturing around the conference room. Gabe admired the Christmas decorations. The red and green streamers, miniature tree in the corner, and snowflakes hanging from the ceiling. "Actually, Lorlaine did an excellent job. I think it adds a lot of holiday cheer."

"Ugh, you would have noticed the Christmas decor. I was talking about the bank itself."

He shrugged. "I'm good with numbers."

"Yeah, but do you *love* it?"

"Does anyone?"

Her eyebrows lifted.

"Okay, fine. My dad and Noel live, eat, and breathe this stuff." He stabbed his catfish with the fork. "I know my strengths and that's the direction I went in."

"If you could do anything you wanted, no limits, no expectations to fulfill, what would you do?"

Gabe drew in a breath. Wasn't that the question he'd been wondering lately? Other than wanting to share his life with a special someone, he had no idea if he wanted a career change. Banking was easy. Banking was stable. Banking put money in his pocket. What else was there?

"I have no idea."

Shanée looked at the man before her. When she first met him, she'd assumed he was one of those overly confident people who went around trying to force people to be as upbeat and confident as him. Yet the more she examined him, the more she realized the façade hid a host of secrets.

Right then, he looked a little lost and uncertain, and that did something funny to her insides. Made a little crack in the shield she'd been wielding since he first smiled at her. Now, she wanted to find out his likes and dislikes and help give him a little direction.

Don't go there, Mitchell. Stick to yourself. It's the best way to handle life.

Instead of taking the opening he'd offered, she closed the door and went back to her to-do list. The rest of their lunch passed quickly, and before she could blink, Shanée was back in her office, peering at the new clock on the wall—black with scripted roman numerals. The short hand pointed to the five and she exited out of her work and logged off for the day.

Shanée powered up her cell as she walked to her car. The brisk wind had her pulling the tie of her wrap coat tighter. It looked like D.C. was moving away from fall temperatures and sliding solidly into winter. Which meant she'd have to break out her coat from when she was stationed in Colorado.

She shuddered as memories of sterile white hospital walls beckoned for attention. Visitors had come and gone, assuring she'd be okay. Even the chaplain had stopped by to offer prayer.

But You forgot to tell the chaplain You don't talk to me.

Her lips pursed. And she *shouldn't* be talking to Him either. She still couldn't figure out why God had abandoned her in her time of need. Why He hadn't given her healing when she'd prayed for it. Why she still had to go to physical therapy for the awful pain she suffered with.

Why? Just why?

Shanée opened her car door. Carefully, she lowered herself onto the seat, thankful the crossover vehicle wasn't as low as a sedan and not as high up as a regular SUV. When she'd realized she wasn't returning back to full speed, she'd sold her beloved Toyota Highlander for something lower, but not low enough to have her stuck with no way of climbing out. She swiveled her feet into the car and closed the door.

She blew out a breath and put her purse on the seat next to her, locking the door before starting the ignition even though the automatic locks would do their job once she reached ten miles an hour. A person could never be too careful. It was one reason why she'd already scanned her interior before even unlocking the door.

As she drove away from Cornwall & Lewis, her cell phone rang, lighting up the navigation system with the caller ID. She groaned. She didn't want to talk to her parents. They were hovering over her like Huey helicopters. Still, she pressed the answer key on her steering wheel and cleared her throat.

"Hello?"

"Hi, how are you?"

Shanée swallowed at the sound of her dad's voice. They were doing good cop, bad cop now? This wasn't good. "I'm fine, Dad. You caught me just as I was driving away from work."

"You enjoying the new job?"

She rolled her eyes but tried to temper her rising irritation. Somewhere, deep down maybe, her dad probably did want to know if she liked her job. But she could smell a setup a mile away. "I haven't been there long enough to tell."

"Well, just do your best, and I'm sure everything will work out."

"Mm hm." She tapped the wheel, turning down the street. Already the roads were filled with cars. Sometimes she thought about catching the Metro instead of driving in to work, especially since she lived near a station in Virginia. But she didn't want to be jostled on a train and not be guaranteed a seat. She'd drive with the rest of the commuters heading to Virginia or Maryland.

"Just wanted to check on you."

"Thanks, Dad." Maybe it really was just a hello.

Dad cleared his throat. "Um, how's the back?"

There it was, the reason for his call. "The same as yesterday." She gripped the steering wheel.

"No relief?"

"I'm okay, Dad." She wanted her heating pad and massage recliner, but she was fine.

"I'm glad you're all right."

Rustling met her ears, and she strained to hear the whispered words her mother was saying.

"Your mom wants to talk to you."

I knew it! She slapped the steering wheel. "Have a good evening, Dad." No use taking her anger out on the good cop.

"Hello, Shanée dear."

"Hi, Mom."

"How was your day?"

She wanted to tell her mother to just get it over with. Drop whatever hand grenade she carried and let the pieces fall where they may. But for some reason, her mother insisted on being nice first.

And didn't that make Shanée sound like the Grinch?

"It was productive."

"Good! I'm so glad to hear that. Are you liking your job?"

She shrugged. "It's a job."

"I'm sure you'll be great at it."

She hoped so, because even though she wasn't in the military any longer, excellence in all she did was still the motto to live by.

"So there was a reason we were calling."

And here it was. "Oh yeah? What's up?"

"We'd love to come out there and visit you."

Shanée's mouth dried. The last time her parents had *visited* was when she'd gotten out of the hospital. After three months, she'd kicked them out. Her mother had been hurt, but if they had hovered and asked her one more time if she was okay, she would have screamed. And by *kicked out*, she meant politely asked them to go home. More than once. She had to insist she was fine even knowing she wasn't. Finally, a tête-à-tête with her dad met her objective when he insisted they return home. Mom hadn't been too happy, but she followed. Guess Shanée made Dad the bad cop at times.

"When were you thinking of visiting?" *And for how long?!*

"Well, it's almost December."

Tomorrow was the first day of the month, but who was keeping track? Apparently, her mother. "Yes. And?"

"And it's the Christmas season. You're in a new city, state, region, and we want to visit."

She could only hope her mom didn't expect to sightsee. Just the thought of walking the miles between the different monuments in D.C., in the cold, in these horrid shoes, was enough to make her want to cry. Instead, she gripped the wheel until her knuckles stiffened.

"For how long?" She wanted to applaud herself at the neutral tone.

"Maybe a couple of weeks?"

"So you want to come a little before Christmas? Until just after New Year's?" She needed concrete details to prepare herself for the abundance of "love" her mother would shower on her in the form of following behind her and making sure she didn't hurt herself or need anything.

"If we come the week of Christmas then we could leave after New Year's. That would be a little over two weeks."

Shanée could live with that. "Okay. Make sure you fly into Dulles."

"Oh, not Ronald Reagan?"

"I work in D.C. but don't live there, Mom."

"Right. Okay. Your father will handle tickets and whatnot."

"All right. If you guys plan on seeing the sights, you'll probably need a rental car. I drive in to work."

"You don't take public transportation?"

Her nose wrinkled. "And risk not having a seat?"

"You're right. Those are so uncomfortable. Maybe your father and I can endure though, so we don't have to get a rental."

"If you want. I do live near a Metro stop."

"Okay. I'll call again with our information."

"Talk to you then, Mom."

"I love you, Shanée."

She smiled. As much as her mother drove her crazy since the accident, she was still her mom. "I love you too."

Chapter Three

Wasn't thirty-one a little old for a twin party? Yet here Gabe stood in the backyard surrounded by friends and family who'd come to wish him and Angel a happy birthday. At least this was better than their tenth birthday party when his mom had gotten the awful idea of doing a Christmas angel theme celebration.

She'd given wings to every guest and had angel-inspired games like *put the wings on the cherubim*. There had also been *Hark the Herald* musical chairs. It had been an embarrassment to both him and Angel and a source of teasing entertainment for their childhood friends for years to come.

Guess that's what happened when a Christmas fanatic finally bore children in December, and twins at that. He and Angel never stood a chance. Thankfully, Gabe had been blessed with a normal name. *Thank You, Lord!* Besides, no one needed to know the A in his middle initial stood for Angel. Gabriel A. Lewis looked inconspicuous unless a person knew that his twin was Angel Gabriel or aligned his moniker with his siblings' names as well. No hiding the Christmas inspired names then.

He took a sip of *heavenly* punch, some concoction his mom had probably found on Pinterest and renamed if she didn't like their proposed title. His sister, Eve, had mentioned there was Elfish punch as well. His mom always had alcohol-free beverages for all guests and made sure everything could be linked back to Christmas.

At least now she wasn't requiring them to dress up like cherubs or seraphim in God's Army like their thirteenth party. The childhood friends he maintained contact with still made cracks about his mom's ideas.

Yet as he gazed around the backyard, Gabe couldn't find any of his friends. All he recognized were his family and a few people he assumed were Angel's new friends from the church she'd been going to with Bishop. Thankfully she'd ditched the superficial ones that used to come around.

"Happy Birthday, Son."

Gabe turned and smiled at his dad. "Thanks."

"I just want you to know your mom wanted a DJ." Dad smirked. "I convinced her streaming music was good enough."

Gabe shuddered. "I owe you." He still remembered that awful DJ she'd hired for their eighteenth birthday. The man had specialized in children's parties—which his mom hadn't realized—and played nothing but kid songs the entire night. His face heated remembering the humiliation.

Dad laughed. "Gotta love your mother and her enthusiasm for Christmas."

That or become embittered. But Gabe would always choose joy. Plus, that path made it easy to make jokes. "She becomes slightly unbalanced over the holidays."

"Maybe, but did you taste those cookies she dropped off at work?" Dad kissed his fingers. "Pure perfection. It's a wonder I don't carry a spare tire." He patted his flat stomach.

Hopefully Dad would pass those tire-fighting genes to Gabe because he couldn't say no to his mom's cookies. He nudged Dad. "That's because you sleep in the gym." It was an inside joke from the one time Gabe had caught Dad sleeping on the weight bench in their basement.

Dad claimed he'd come down to work out and changed his mind. Angel had declared the bench cushier than the tufted sofa in their living room and therefore a much better place to sleep after a fight. Not that his parents ever did.

"There might be some truth to that. Gotta do something when you have insomnia."

Gabe raised his brows. "How about retire and learn how to sleep?"

"I don't think Noel is ready."

And I was never an option, was I? But Gabe didn't examine the feeling that arose at the mention of his saintly brother. Instead, he scanned the backyard for Saint Noel. The white lights strewn about gave the space a holiday feel, and the red and white decor his mother had used added to the atmosphere. Still, he didn't see his brother in the crowd.

"Where *is* Noel?"

"He had to change. I told him he could borrow a sweater."

Just then Lorlaine stepped in front of them, a cup of heavenly punch in her hand. "Happy birthday, Gabe. Where's that sister of yours?"

"Thanks, Lorlaine." He smiled and pointed toward the makeshift dance floor in their yard. "She's on the dance floor with Marvel."

Lorlaine turned and placed a hand on her heart. "Well, isn't that precious? I just love their little family."

So do I. Once again that desire for more arose within. Gabe wished he could talk to Dad about it, or Noel, or . . . someone, but he also didn't want to see the expressions on their faces. The accusatory comments of why he felt a lack when he'd been so blessed.

He had a good job working at Cornwall & Lewis. A nice car. Even owned his own home. Granted it was in various stages of being renovated, but it was his, nonetheless. He was a catch, to use Mom's word.

Yet the women he went out with had never created that desire in him to continue the relationship. His siblings may have teased him for breaking hearts, but honestly, he didn't date women long enough to *break* their hearts. No use stringing someone along in hopes that a special feeling would come about when it was obvious from the get-go that no spark existed.

Was he being shallow? Should he date someone longer to see if feelings would eventually materialize? Or was the idea of a spark-and-fireworks type of attraction all a myth?

"Well, I'll see you two later."

"Bye, Lorlaine," Gabe said.

"I'll walk you out," Dad offered.

A flash of something bright caught Gabe's eye. He straightened, craning his neck, trying to keep the peek of color in his view. *There!* A glint of silky blue snagged his attention. As he walked toward it, he realized it was a woman's outfit. Long flowing black hair fell down a woman's back. The blue silk shirt and black pencil skirt accentuated her feminine curves. Someone took his mom's dress code to heart.

Sure, he was wearing a suit minus the tie—he choked enough at work—but he didn't expect the guests to dress to the nines just because Carol Lewis demanded it. Her sophisticated Christmas theme didn't soften the blow of a double birthday party with his twin sister.

He caught a glimpse of the woman whose skin tone reminded him of the paint his mom used to decorate the basement. It had that weird name that made him think of a horse. What was it again? *Sorrel.* He grinned and maneuvered himself to be in a position to see the woman face to face as soon as his mother stopped talking her ear off.

Gabe went over opening lines in his head and stepped forward. "Sorry to interrupt, Mom, but have you seen Noel?"

Not his smoothest excuse for an interruption but it made the women pause from their talking. The mystery woman straightened and slowly turned. Gabe held his breath and almost choked on the shock of who stood before him.

"Shanée?"

Her lips formed into a practiced smile. "Happy Birthday, Gabe."

"Shanée?"

She arched an eyebrow. "I don't look that different without my glasses."

Yes, she did, but who was he to argue? Instead, he noted the deep brown color of her eyes, the bloom in her cheeks, and her gorgeous hair. Oh man, why did the first spark he felt toward someone have to be caused by Shanée Mitchell?

Shanée studied Gabe. Was he sick? He kept opening and shutting his mouth. She took a step back in case he decided to upchuck that suspicious looking drink all over her. What was in the cocktail? Looked like sherbet fell into some liquid and everyone decided to drink it anyway. And what was with the candy cane sticking out of his cup?

When Mr. Lewis had invited her to his home to celebrate Gabe and his sister's birthday, Shanée had immediately declined. Respectfully, of course, but a no, nevertheless. Only Mr. Lewis hadn't left it at that. He'd assured her that she wouldn't be the only employee to attend. His invitation had almost sounded like a mandate, but not enough for her to definitely come to that conclusion. Instead of continuing to decline, she agreed. After being here for a few minutes, she'd already spotted other coworkers. Guess the boss had been right.

Still, she felt incredibly awkward standing in the glamorous backyard that belonged to her employer. And the way Gabe's mom fawned all over her shot matchmaking hints in the air. She could only hope that something would distract the woman. Maybe the look on Gabe's face would catch his mother's attention.

"Noel is talking to your dad." Mrs. Lewis gestured toward the gazebo at the edge of the yard, lit up like something in a Hallmark Christmas movie right before the hero and heroine finally kissed.

Not that she knew anything about Hallmark Christmas movies. The desire to believe in happily ever after had been shelved like her beautiful strappy espadrilles that would look a whole lot better than the flats she'd chosen for this outfit. They weren't as ugly as her work shoes, but they certainly weren't as pretty as the peep toe blue suede shoes in her closet.

She suppressed a sigh as images of dancing in gorgeous heels flitted through her head. Her dancing days were over. Basically, anything that had once brought her enjoyment was gone thanks to her back issues. Still, she kept her lips curved in a smile that said she was paying attention. Hopefully Gabe and his mother would miss the *couldn't care less* expression on her face.

"Are you ill, Gabe?" Mrs. Lewis asked.

Gabe's mouth snapped shut, and he shook his head. But the poleaxed expression he'd been wearing had yet to fade.

Shanée grimaced. "Maybe it's the drink?" She pointed to the foamy concoction. "Is it upsetting your stomach?'

His mom gasped. "Oh no. Everyone's been drinking it. What am I going to do?" she whispered, but the last question ended on a wail.

It was all so dramatic but genuine. Mrs. Lewis really did love Christmas to be perfect. Shanée hoped the woman never had her bubble burst.

"It's not the drink, Mom. I'm fine."

"You don't look it," she declared.

Shanée agreed. She still thought he was going to lose his lunch.

He blew out a breath, and Shanée hopped backward. She bit back a word as pain shot down her leg. She hissed, sucking in air and trying to appear as if everything was perfectly normal. But judging by the twin stares of concern, she hadn't been successful.

"Are *you* okay?" Gabe asked softly.

She wanted to nod, but that might set off another reaction in her back. Dang spine. Why did it have to have so many nerves? Just one mild misalignment and nerve pain was her new best frenemy.

"I'm fine," she gritted. She placed a palm against her lower back, breathing steadily and waiting for the sting to reside.

"You don't look fine, Shanée."

"Goodness, neither one of you do. Go inside. Gabe, get this girl some pain medicine or something."

"Yes, ma'am."

"But be back out in a half hour. We'll do cake."

"No ice cream?" Shanée muttered, clenching her jaw.

"There will be ice cream too, Ms. Mitchell." His mom smiled and walked away.

Gabe gestured toward the white brick house. "Can you walk?"

"Yes." But some days she wondered if using a wheelchair would bring relief. Then guilt would assault her. There were people out there who literally *couldn't* walk. How could she justify the use of a wheelchair, even if the thought brought imagined relief?

Gabe slid both hands into his pockets after ditching his drink on a nearby tray. "Want to tell me what happened? Did you step wrong? Get cramps?"

She arched an eyebrow his way.

"I have three sisters, remember?"

"If I did get cramps, I would never admit it."

He nodded gravely. "So do you need some Midol?"

"Please stop talking."

He flashed that grin, and a hint of a dimple winked through the scruff growing on his face. Somehow, he managed to look put together despite the lack of shaving. Being in the Air Force for so long had her admiring clean-cut guys left and right. Gabe was slowly upending those preferences with his dark eyes, manly scruff, and positive demeanor.

Shanée diverted her gaze and eyed the home's interior. Turquoise blue and silver streamers hung from the walls but not in a gaudy way. How did Mrs. Lewis do it?

"Your mother has exquisite taste."

"Yes. My dad always jokes and says that's the reason he became a banker."

"Did you wear braces?"

"What?" Gabe blinked, staring at her bemusedly. "I did. Why?"

She shook her head, her cheeks flushing from the foolish question. "No reason."

Gabe showed her to the living room, and she took in the tufted couch cushions. They looked firm enough to bring relief to her back. She slid her hand under her skirt and cautiously lowered herself. A sigh fell from her lips as tension she hadn't realized she'd carried seeped out of her. "This is wonderful."

"You *like* this?" Gabe's mouth dropped open. "She sold our old couch for this monstrosity. It's so hard."

"Just what my back needs."

He sat down across from her, arms resting on his thighs. "What happened to your back?"

She eyed him, wondering if she should come clean. Before she could come to a decision, heels clacked across the hardwood floor and a beautiful woman entered the room.

Her black hair had been parted in the middle and hung straight down. Her brown skin glowed and she smiled at Gabe. Was this his girlfriend? She was certainly pretty enough. Shanée couldn't imagine Gabe dating someone who didn't match him in looks. But when she talked to him, Shanée didn't get the vibe he was that shallow.

"Gabriel, happy birthday," the woman cried. He stood and wrapped his arms around the petite female.

Shanée's stomach twisted. Why did her chest burn all of a sudden? She hadn't had any of that punch.

"I can't believe you're thirty-one, little brother."

Little brother? Shanée sat up straighter, thankful the sudden movement didn't tweak her back again. This was one of his sisters?

"Eve, meet Shanée Mitchell. She recently started working at the bank."

Eve beamed at Shanée. "Nice to meet you. Have you been listening to Gabe's antics?"

He snorted. "I've been a perfect gentleman. She didn't feel well, so we were relaxing away from the crowd."

"Mm hm. Sure." Eve winked at Shanée.

"I'm serious, Eve. We're coworkers." He rubbed a hand over the back of his head. "Hey, Shanée, I'm sure my sister has some pain meds if you need any."

Shanée shook her head. She had enough in her purse for *just in case* purposes. "I'm okay. Sitting helped." She rose slowly. She needed to get out of there. Suddenly her tear ducts seemed to want to resurrect as *we're coworkers* rang in her head.

She wasn't sure why that bothered her so much, but it did for some reason, and now she wanted to be alone.

"I'm going to go back outside. Thanks, Gabe."

She returned to the outdoor party and discreetly made her way out the back fence and to her car. She drove away from a lifestyle that could never be hers.

Chapter Four

Gabe trotted down the stairs in his parents' house. He'd chosen to sleep over last night after the party ended versus driving back to Virginia in the middle of the night. Plus, his mom always made a nice spread for breakfast. Judging by the smell of sausage wafting in the air, he'd been right.

He stepped onto the ground floor and made his way to the kitchen. He blinked, surprised by the vision before him. Dad and Mom were dancing like they were at the prom. Literally. Dancing. His father did some move that had his mom twirling out then he pulled her close to him again. They swayed back and forth to Boyz II Men singing "Let it Snow."

Gabe's face heated and he stepped back, right into the china cabinet. A dish clanked against another. He rounded to ensure nothing fell. *Phew, that was close.* When he turned back around, his parents were still swaying to the music but now had their eyes on him.

Gabe cleared his throat. "Oops."

"No worries. Come on in, Son," Dad said. He looked down at Gabe's mother with adoration.

Gabe wanted to exit stage left and get out of there. He checked his wristwatch, and his mouth gaped. "Dad, do you know what time it is?"

"I do."

"It's nine." Gabe stared at his father. What was he doing at home still? Sure, it was a Saturday but that had never kept him home before.

"Today's our anniversary," Mom said. She sighed, laying her head on Dad's chest.

Gabe's brow furrowed. "I thought your anniversary was in June."

"Our wedding anniversary is," Dad said.

Okay. He had no clue they celebrated more than one anniversary. And although embarrassment came off him in waves at the obvious affection between them, he couldn't help but be a tad envious too.

"Is Angel awake?" Mom asked as the song ended.

"Yes. I believe Marvel woke her up."

"Good. Then they should be coming down for breakfast." She smiled at him. "Hungry?"

"Starved."

Mom rolled her eyes. "Always eating, Gabriel Angel."

"Mom . . ." he warned.

"I can call you by your first and middle name if I want." She popped a hip. "Mother's prerogative."

He sighed. "Does the dining table need to be set up?"

"Your father already did it."

Gabe eyed his dad.

"Son, you're going to give me a complex. You act like I'm never home."

"You're not when he's around, dear." Mom blew Dad a kiss.

"Eww," Angel said as she came to stand next to him. "Why are they being so lovey dovey?" she muttered.

He chuckled, glad someone understood his pain. "They claim it's an anniversary."

"They got married in June."

"That's what I said."

"What anniversary are you celebrating?" Angel asked as she sauntered further into the room. She'd obviously come prepared to spend the night. Gone was the green gown from last night. Now she wore a black wrap dress and red high heels.

Gabe peered over his shoulder into the hallway just in time to see his brother-in-law come down the stairs with Marvel. "Morning, Bishop."

"Morning, Uncle Gabe," Marvel shouted, flying down the steps. She stopped in front of him. "Are you old too now?"

His brows rose. "I didn't know I was old."

"That's what Mom said. She said she's old and the rest of her years will be downhill from here."

"Why would she say that?"

Marvel parroted matter-of-factly, "Because I asked why she was dressed so pretty for the weekend."

Gabe laughed and high-fived Marvel. She gave an impish shrug of her shoulders. When Gabe turned back into the kitchen, his family had already started gathering dishes to bring into the dining room. Bishop grabbed the casserole from Angel.

"Angel, which anniversary did they say they were celebrating?"

A whoosh of cold air blasted them, and he turned to see the front door wide open and the rest of his siblings coming in. Well, everyone except Noel. He was probably slumped over his desk at work since Dad had chosen to stay home.

He hugged Eve and Starr, then shook Waylon's hand.

"Who's celebrating what?" Eve asked.

"Mom and Dad," Angel replied. "Apparently they're celebrating the first time they said *I love you*."

"Aww." Starr placed a hand on her heart while her husband, Waylon, shook his head in amusement.

"You wouldn't have said *aww* if you would have seen them making eyes at each other." Gabe slid his hands into his pockets. "The level of affection in the kitchen was way too much for so early in the day."

"Boy, it's nine o'clock." Eve shoved his shoulder.

He contorted his face into a look of mock outrage, but she just laughed. He'd always led a life of making his siblings laugh. No one ever thought he was serious. But last night, when he'd discovered Shanée had disappeared, he'd lost his natural good humor. The change in his countenance had been so noticeable, Noel had asked him what was wrong. Not willing to share what had been on his mind, he'd cracked a joke about the lack of theme for the birthday party and redirected the conversation.

Only now she was once more back in his thoughts. Had she felt that slight flicker of attraction yesterday? Probably not. Gabe didn't look too much different than he did at work. But the veil had come down for her and he saw her clearly now. Not that he was only into good looks.

I hope that doesn't make me shallow, Lord. But I'm not sorry that I've seen her in a new light. Just not sure what to do about it.

So today, he'd hang out with his family and put thoughts of Shanée Mitchell away. Besides, his parents probably had some family fun planned now that the calendar had flipped to December. While they kicked off the decorations with the Thanksgiving holiday, they didn't start the festivities until the last month of the year. His mom always used his and Angel's birthday to kick off a month of Christmas fun.

The family gathered around the dining table.

"Honey, would you say grace?" Mom asked.

Dad nodded, bowing his head. "Thank you for this time together as a family and for my bride. Amen." On the chorus of *amens*, serving dishes were passed one by one. Everything looked so good that Gabe took a helping of each item.

"Let's hear it," Angel said.

"Hear what, Angel Gabrielle?" Mom asked.

Gabe smirked at the use of her first and middle names. Mom really was in a mood. Would she do it with the others? Although Noel was the only one who hadn't been saddled with a ridiculous middle name. Probably because his first name was a pain with everyone assuming he was a girl.

"What you have planned for this season."

Mom stared at Dad and his lips curved. But instead of causing Gabe to fake gag, or even inspire a twinge of *someday* wishing, their covert glances pooled dread in his middle.

"Uh oh. What's that look mean?" He gestured between the two of them.

Eve dropped a fork and squinted at the 'rents. "What's going on?"

"Your dad and I have decided to go on a vacation."

"What?" Angel cried.

His thoughts exactly. They never went anywhere during Christmas unless it was mandated family fun.

"Well, your father is always so busy with the bank that we don't get a lot of time to vacation alone."

"But we always celebrate the holidays together," Eve said. Her lower lip trembled.

"Now Eve Estelle, don't go piling on the guilt," Mom said. "You all are in your thirties."

"Not me," Starr quipped.

Dad cleared his throat. "Some of you even have families of your own. We can't get together every holiday."

"Sure we can. We *always* do, Mom." Gabe snapped his mouth shut. He didn't want to sound like a petulant child when he literally just celebrated turning thirty-one, but why now? He eyed his dad. "Are you sick?"

"What?" Dad shook his head. "Gabriel, I'm old. I want to slow down and not work so much."

"No, I think Gabe's right," Eve interjected. "You're usually at work by now and all of a sudden you and Mom want to take a vacation?" She crossed her arms. "I don't believe it."

"Believe this," Mom snapped. "We're going on vacation. We'll be back Christmas Day."

"And we expect you to get together and carry out our traditions," Dad said.

"But . . ." Starr looked down at her plate, sadness drawing her mouth downward.

Gabe looked around the table at his siblings. He cleared his throat. "We've been waiting for them to go away for forever. We finally get the house to ourselves. I smell a good Christmas party coming."

Eve chuckled and met his gaze. "A party *before* they return at that."

"Amen," Angel said. She nudged Starr.

Starr looked at Waylon, who gave her a reassuring nod, then the rest of them. "Party it is."

"Oh, look what we started, babe," Mom muttered.

"Let them have their fun. We'll be having ours."

"Sick," the rest of them groused as their parents kissed.

Shanée's fingers flew across the keyboard as she typed up her initial findings for Cornwall & Lewis. She'd received an email to turn the report into Gabe instead of Mr. Lewis. Apparently, the boss was going on vacation. That information must have already spread because that was all her coworkers were talking about in the break room earlier.

A knock sounded on her door, and she lifted her gaze from the computer to the doorway where Gabe stood looking concerned.

She bit back a groan. Would he ask about her back? Demand to know what happened? Or worse, turn those puppy dog eyes of pity on her?

Fortunately, her masseuse had been able to see her over the weekend and work out the kinks in her back. That, and her heating pad had been her friend. She felt as good as she was going to get this Monday morning.

"Hey. Did you need something?" She pointed toward her computer. "I'm typing up the initial feedback right now."

Gabe waved a hand. "No, no. I didn't come in here to micromanage. I actually wanted to," he looked out in the hall then stepped over the threshold, lowering his voice. "Wanted to check on you. And invite you to a party."

Her mouth dropped. A party? Like a *date?* Her pulse skyrocketed at the idea. "What kind of party?"

A huge grin covered his face. "Our parents are going out of town so me and the sibs decided to throw a party. Sort of a late teenage rebellion type deal."

She forced a chuckle at the realization that he wasn't asking her as a date. Not that she *wanted* to date Gabe Lewis. So what if she found him attractive. "That sounds kind of fun. When is it?"

"We're going to do it Christmas Eve."

"Did you invite everyone else already?" *Or just me?*

"Actually, you were my first stop."

She would completely ignore the shiver of pleasure at that thought. "Oh. I'd like to come." Especially since Mr. Lewis wouldn't be there. She felt entirely awkward at the birthday party, but a regular old party sounded just fine. "Is there a theme?"

"Christmas." His lips curved in a half smile as if to say *what else?*

"Makes sense. Being as y'all all have Christmas names."

He cocked his head. "Y'all? Was that a hint of an accent I heard, Ms. Mitchell?"

Her face flushed. "No." Hadn't traveling all over the world while serving erased her origins? Her mom always complained she couldn't hear Shanée's accent anymore. She'd worked hard to ensure that people would judge her on her work ethics, not her gender, where she came from, or who she may or may not know.

"Mm hm. I'll let it go." He took another step farther into her office. "Besides, I'm hoping you'll tell me how your back is."

Shanée locked eyes with Gabe, her breath hitching in her chest. "It's fine," she squeaked. She coughed, trying to cover up her embarrassment. "I'm fine."

His eyes darted back and forth, roaming her features and probably trying to detect any lies. "If you weren't, would you tell me?"

"Probably not." She said it swiftly and, hopefully, not abrasively.

He nodded slowly, as if assessing the situation or determining how he felt about her answer. Gabe took a few more steps and stopped in front of her desk. "What could I do to change that?"

"What?" She blinked. What did he mean?

"I mean, how can I become a confidant? A person you'd actually tell if your back was bothering you?"

She stared at him, unsure of how to answer. Because, truth was, she didn't talk about her pain to anyone. Well, there were her medical professionals she saw and to whom she candidly described her suffering. She wanted them to treat her and make her better, so they needed to know. But outside of doctors and nurses, no one knew just how much the pain plagued her.

"I don't even know how to answer that," she replied honestly.

Gabe sat in her chair. "Okay. How about this. Every December, my brothers and sisters and I get together for different festivities. Tonight, we're going to a place that does epic hot chocolate. You make your own and then they give you supplies to make some as a Christmas gift. Will you join me?"

Shanée's heart pounded. Be with others for Christmas? Participate in events that celebrated the season? Her stomach curdled, like month-old milk. "I don't know, Gabe."

"Please. It's a sit-down affair, so no standing unless you want to. They do have stations where you can stand if you prefer, but I'll make sure you're comfortable."

It wasn't his job but sweet of him to offer. Besides, she was never without lumbar support. Because she'd yet to go to a restaurant where the chairs were comfortable.

"You're still quiet," Gabe quipped. "Thinking of how to let me down easy, huh?"

Shanée resisted the urge to laugh when Gabe poked his lower lip out. "I was thinking."

"Thinking yes?" he asked.

If she said no, would he invite her to something else? "Can I think about it some more?" *Because you don't think enough things to death.*

"Sure." He rose. "Just let me know before I walk out the door today." He tapped the doorjamb. "I could give you my cell phone number if you want. That way you can text me if you're coming and I can send you directions." He paused. "Or pick you up?"

Nope. This sounded too much like a date. Shanée cleared her throat. "You can text me the address. I have GPS." She smiled to take the sting out of her words. Still, she wanted him to know she wasn't interested in getting closer.

At least not yet.

No, not at all. Office romances were a huge no-no. Plus, the holiday atmosphere was messing with her, softening her. It was like every carol on the radio, all the decorations, and even Gabe himself were plotting to get her to throw her head back and sing around a Christmas tree.

Nope, not going to happen. She would do her job, go home, and repeat.

Chapter Five

A gust of cold air blew against the door as Gabe held it open for his family. While his brothers and sisters—and their spouses—entered Heaven (the dessert bar), Gabe scanned the people walking by. Surely Shanée would be among them. She'd texted him ten minutes ago and let him know she was on the way. He didn't know what changed her mind, but he was grateful.

Lord, please let her have fun tonight. Oh, and could you make sure my brothers and sisters don't get too out of hand? He knew they'd embarrass him. It was a rite of passage, a tradition probably dating back to the first pair of siblings to walk the earth.

He grimaced. *That's a bad analogy.* He didn't have any Cain-Abel thoughts towards the sibs. He loved them and wanted the best for them. He also wasn't opposed to throwing in some good-natured jabs when it came to the romance department. But if he wasn't careful, the tables would turn the moment Shanée walked through the door. Whenever that happened, seeing as there was no sign of her now.

He let the door close behind him and followed Angel's retreating back toward their reserved table. Eve or Noel had most likely made the reservations. The two hated to wait around for anything, including Christmas festivities. They'd always been the whiniest of the bunch but would claim Starr lived up to her youngest status and was actually the neediest. Considering she was an author who'd hit a couple of bestsellers lists, Gabe would move her from the *just living* side to the *living it up* column. The rest of them needed to step up their game. Oh wait, Angel had already hit magazine stands with her interior design skills.

"Gabe?"

He whirled around, and light filled his chest at the sight of his new coworker. "Hey. You made it." He lessened the gap between them and hooked a finger over his shoulder. "They just went to sit down."

"I'm not late?" Her brow wrinkled.

"Not at all. Glad you could make it."

She nodded cautiously. "Thanks for inviting me."

This was awkward. Nothing like manners dictated by parents of old to increase the weirdness of seeing each other outside of work. But Gabe would thaw the ice. He had to. "Follow me, all right?"

"Sure."

He led the way, sliding his hands into his peacoat pockets. Gabe wanted to place his hand on the small of Shanée's back and let her lead, but she had no clue where they usually sat. Yet every instinct in him shouted to assist her and make sure she was at ease. He glanced over his shoulder and offered a reassuring smile before facing forward once more.

A few seconds later, he turned down the hall and came to a stop at their table. "Hey, guys, this is Shanée Mitchell. She's going to join us tonight." The crew waved and said assorted greetings. Gabe pointed to them one by one, going down the right side of the table before coming up the left. "This is Eve. Noel. Angel and her husband, Bishop."

Shanée gave a little wave as he continued.

"And Waylon and his wife, AKA my sister, Starr. And we can take these two empty spots." Fortunately, Waylon and Starr had left the first two chairs open. Gabe sat next to Starr, allowing Shanée to sit at the head of the table. He wasn't sure if that would be comfortable and he tried not to stare as she slipped a lumbar pillow—which he'd mistaken as a tote—onto the chair before sitting.

"I've never been to this place."

"It's the best for desserts. Hence the name Heaven," Eve explained.

"So, they sell desserts, not just hot chocolate?"

"Oh yes," Angel remarked. "You've got to taste their fudge."

"No, the molten lava cake," Starr quipped.

"How about the cheesecake?" Eve asked.

The ladies broke out in rapid conversation as they discussed the best dessert on the menu. Gabe shook his head and caught Noel's eye across the table, then Bishop's. Noel looked like he wanted to run for the hills, and Bishop stared at Angel with affection.

It would be nauseating if Gabe wasn't so happy that Angel was with a good man. She and Starr had lucked out in that department, especially considering the bullet they'd both dodged when they'd dated the same guy. Gabe still wished he would have punched Ashton's lights out.

He blew out a breath.

"Are you okay?" Shanée asked.

He looked at her beautiful brown eyes. "Got caught up in a bad memory." He offered a smile. "I'm good now. Thanks."

"I can understand that."

"Anything you want to share?" He held his breath.

Shanée met his gaze then looked down. "Not in this setting."

"You name the time and place, and I'll listen."

"Thank you, Gabe."

He nodded just as their server came by. Noel took charge as he usually did.

"We'd like to order desserts and the hot chocolate bomb kit."

"Great." The woman gave Noel a sultry smile. "For you and your wife," she pointed to Eve, "Or the whole table."

"The whole table," he answered smoothly, evading the woman's attempt to find out his marital status.

"Let's start with you. I bet you want something sweet."

Angel made a gagging motion but covered the side of her mouth so the server wouldn't notice. Gabe stared at his menu, trying not to laugh. Noel never had a difficult time finding a woman to date, but he never went with the ones screaming desperation either.

They all ordered and soon the server was back with their desserts. "Would you like the hot chocolate bomb kits now or after you eat?"

"After, please," Shanée said.

The woman looked disappointed that Noel didn't answer but took the hint and went to the next table in her section.

"Thanks. She wasn't taking the hint," Noel said.

"No problem. Although your wife should have spoken up," Shanée grinned at the disgust curling Eve's lip.

"I've got to get a boyfriend. Everyone keeps thinking I'm dating my brother." She shuddered while the rest of the table laughed.

Well Gabe did. Angel and Starr gave sympathetic glances to the two oldest. "Doesn't help that you two always dress alike."

Eve looked down. "I'm wearing my clothes from work."

"Exactly. Noel always wears a suit, and you wear the feminine equivalent."

"She looks good," Angel defended.

"Professional," added Starr.

"As does Noel," Gabe said. "Hence why people always think they're together. They're the very image of a powerhouse couple."

"You're just jealous. Everyone always assumes you're single." Angel stuck her tongue out at him.

"Afraid of commitment?" Shanée asked.

His face heated.

"He is," his sisters chimed.

Noel stifled a laugh, taking a bite of his tiramisu.

"I'm not afraid of commitment," Gabe stared into Shanée's eyes. Because as far as he was concerned, she was the only one who needed to know. "I just haven't found the right woman yet."

Shanée's stomach let loose the caged butterflies. There was no way Gabe was insinuating *she* could be the right woman. They didn't even *know* each other.

I mean, how can I become a confidant? A person you'd actually tell if your back was bothering you?

Though he *had* tried to bridge the gap at work. Before she could think of a comeback—because really, her mind was reeling—Gabe smiled and turned to the decadent dessert he'd ordered. It looked like five layers of various chocolates stacked as a cake. A very chocolaty cake.

As much as Shanée enjoyed chocolate, she couldn't eat it in cake form. Which was why she was very happy with her pumpkin cheesecake.

It also helped to keep her hands occupied so she didn't feel completely awkward with the Lewis family. They asked her questions here and there but nothing overwhelming and nothing too intrusive either. Still, she was very aware of Gabe's presence beside her, the heat coming off him in waves. Maybe it was the sweater he'd changed into after work.

Besides Starr and Shanée, Gabe was the only one dressed down. Everyone else looked like they'd come straight from work. Judging by the teasing directed at Eve and Noel earlier, that was how they dressed all the time.

"So Shanée, where are you from?" Angel asked, peering over the rim of her coffee mug.

Shanée's back spasmed as she reached for her own drink. She kept a neutral expression on her face as she carefully lowered her arm. Despite the lumbar cushion, her spine hadn't loved the seating arrangements.

Back to the matter at hand, Mitchell. She cleared her throat. "Mississippi."

"Really?" Angel leaned forward. "Laurel, Mississippi?"

Eve snorted. "Girl, the state has more than one city."

"Of course it does, but how neat would it be if that was her home town?"

All the men groaned at her nod to the HGTV show. Shanée held back a grin because the tension had temporarily been shifted away from her.

"*Are* you from Laurel?" Noel asked quietly.

"No. A small town not on a map and one that search engines spin that wheel looking for."

"How come you didn't go home for Christmas?" Starr asked.

Because her mom would expect Shanée to pick up life right where she'd left it when she left home after high school. Shanée had no desire to go back working at the local grocer when she'd been able to further her education thanks to Uncle Sam. Plus, she and her mom didn't see eye to eye on everything.

More like nothing.

"This is my home now." Not to mention she'd never been big on Christmas.

The Lewis family all nodded as if that made sense. Honestly, she'd never voiced it out loud and doing so warmed her insides.

"Did you get a place in D.C.?" Eve asked.

"No. Virginia."

"Oh, like Gabe." The eldest sister smiled, exchanging some kind of look with the others.

One that had Shanée wanting to correct their assumptions. But she also didn't want to bring attention to herself. Maybe if she ignored the insinuations, they would fade away in the wind.

"Where are you at?" Shanée asked Gabe.

"I have a place out in Ashburn."

A little too suburban for her taste. McLean was her stopping grounds.

"I bought a fixer upper."

"It even has some acreage," Angel added.

"Really?" She stared at Gabe. "I didn't picture you as the man puttering around his house, fixing things."

He chuckled, and she ignored the pebbled flesh on her arms. Why was his laughter so smooth? He sounded like he practiced for a radio spot.

"I do like to putter around, as you put it. It's relaxing to fix something in the house when I come home."

She snorted. "Sounds like an extended workday."

"That's what I said," Eve chimed in.

"It is kind of relaxing," Waylon stated.

Shanée couldn't remember if he'd spoken up before. He was kind of quiet.

"Agreed," Bishop, Angel's husband, stated. He rubbed her shoulders. "Being able to hammer away your frustrations from the day is therapeutic."

"Guys, always having to break something." But the adoring smile Angel gave Bishop took away any insult to her words. The couple kissed briefly, and Shanée averted her eyes.

Only the two youngest girls were married, but the atmosphere of happiness seemed to cloud over the singles.

"I only have the master bedroom and bathroom to finish," Gabe added.

"You've renovated all the rooms yourself?" she asked.

He nodded.

"Wow. That's amazing." A man who had brains and some brawn. Was that what the sweater was hiding? Muscles? *Get a grip, Mitchell! He's your coworker.*

"Hey, maybe we should do one of our activities at your house," Eve said.

"Speaking of, how does this tradition work?" Shanée asked. "Gabe told me very little."

"Just like him," Starr shook her head. She peered over Gabe's form. "Our mom is a Christmas fanatic and has to celebrate all things Christmas."

"And Dad indulges her," Eve added.

"Yeah, he does," Gabe muttered.

Shanée laughed at his disgruntled look.

"Besides our names, she's always made sure we decorate for the holidays, go to a tree lighting, do something related to food."

"Hence tonight," Angel interjected.

"Right," Starr continued. "So we just do as much Christmas fun as possible. Now that we're all older and have our own lives, we put it in the family calendar so no one misses out."

"So y'all always do things like this? Every year?"

They all nodded.

"Without fail?"

"Without. Fail," Gabe said. "One year we got a stomach flu. As soon as we were all better, Mom bundled us up and hustled us out of the door to the closest activity."

"Didn't we do ice skating that year?" Noel asked.

The Lewis siblings nodded.

Shanée wondered what it would be like to have a Christmas like that. Her parents never had money for presents growing up, so they chose not to celebrate the holiday. By the time Shanée joined the military, she had made her own opinions of the holiday—granted, some were probably steeped in bitterness—and chosen to be the one always working. Not that the U.S. Government would have her work the actual day off; however, while everyone in her office was taking leave to go away on vacation, she worked each day allowed.

The server stopped by with a tray full of goodies. "Here are your kits." She smiled at Noel as she placed a sheet of paper in the middle of the table. "Those are the instructions, but it's pretty basic. Fill one half of the bomb with options from these containers." She placed square containers of nuts, sprinkles, marshmallows, etc. "Then add a little cocoa powder, add the top half, and then decorate the outside." She pointed to number five on the printout. "This tells you how to fuse the two sides together."

"Thank you."

The woman met Shanée's gaze. "My pleasure." Then she glanced over her shoulder and winked at Noel.

Shanée tried to hold in her laugh, but hearing Gabe snicker next to her had her coughing to cover her slip-up. Once the woman was out of earshot, she shot a look at Gabe. "You're a bad influence."

"Ha. That was all her. I'm sure she practiced that look in the mirror."

"It's hard to catch a man's attention," Angel remarked.

Bishop snorted, and she turned to him. "Puh-lease, you purposely ignored me, so you don't count."

The rest of the siblings hooted. Shanée loved how they joked with one another but obviously had each other's back as well. Being an only child, she never had that. Just her and her parents in their two-bedroom home.

Shanée carefully reached for a chocolate mold—thankful her back cooperated—and filled it with cocoa powder and mint chunks. She read the instructions to figure out how to fuse the two halves.

"Need some help?" Gabe asked.

"I think I can do it." Her brow furrowed as she tried to hold the closed halves together.

"Let me help," Gabe suggested quietly.

She huffed. "Fine."

He fused the two halves then handed it back to her. "There you go."

"Thanks, Gabe." She swallowed as her fingertips grazed his. Why was it so hot in there all of a sudden?

"No problem. Want me to do the next one too? I mean, after you fill it."

Shanée looked up, gazing into his warm eyes. Eyes that had told her he wanted to be there for her. All of a sudden, she needed an excuse to leave before she bought into the idea that romance was for her.

She leaned in close. "I'm not sure I can sit anymore. My back," she murmured.

"What would make it better?" he whispered.

"Standing." Because if she didn't get up soon, she might not be able to at all.

"Do you need help?"

As much as she didn't want to ask, she nodded and let Gabe help her. She tried to ignore the warmth of his hand and how protected she felt as he guided her up. Her back spasmed, and all romantic thoughts fled as her eyes teared.

"You're not going to be able to drive home, are you?"

She assessed the pain in her body. "No," she said around the lump in her throat. So much for avoiding him.

"Will you allow me to take you home?"

"Yes." Because she really had no other choice.

But maybe, just maybe, she could still guard her heart against the man intent on breaking down her barriers.

Chapter Six

This was a mistake. He should have never invited Shanée to join him and his siblings. Because of him, she was in pain. The only comfort Gabe could offer her was the heated seats her car provided as he drove her home.

"Are you all right?" he murmured. It was hard to tell if she'd fallen asleep considering the pitch-black night that surrounded them.

"Not yet." She moaned as she shifted in the seat.

Gabe winced, keeping his eyes on the road in front of him despite the overwhelming urge to reach out and offer a hand for comfort. "Is there anything I can do?"

"You're doing it. You didn't have to drive me home. Especially knowing you'll have to take an Uber home."

Noel had offered to drive Gabe's car home and would spend the night at his house. They would carpool to work tomorrow. Which meant they'd have to leave the house under insane conditions: o'dark-thirty while the rest of northern Virginia slept, and Noel could continue his streak as the first person to walk in Cornwall & Lewis's doors.

"It's the least I could do. I really thought you'd be okay at the restaurant."

"I should have gotten up and moved around." She sighed. "Lesson learned."

"What happened, Shanée?" He held his breath, waiting to see if she would trust him.

Please let her trust me. Because somehow, someway, Shanée Mitchell made him want to be the one she'd share secrets with. Not to be Gabe the comedian or Gabe the jokester. He wanted her to see there was more to him just as there was more to her.

"It happened in the military."

His mind jumped, imagining her overseas. Then again, the problem was with her back and improvised explosive devices (IEDs) usually turned soldiers into wounded warriors.

"How bad was it?"

She moaned, shifting once more. "Bad. It all started on a fun day."

A what? "What made it fun?" he asked.

She chuckled. "No, that's what it's called. 'Fun days' are usually a day the squadron commander marks as a way for everyone to go out and have some fun. Fuel the whole esprit de corps and camaraderie."

Huh. "Where did you guys go?"

"Skiing. When I was stationed in Colorado."

He couldn't imagine living somewhere out west. "Did you enjoy Colorado before then?"

"I mean, sure. It was neat to see the mountains and experience the cold. But it never really felt like home. You know?"

Gabe's parents were the epitome of home, so when he went to college then got his own place, it took Gabe a while to feel like he'd created the same environment. Buying the fixer upper in Ashburn had changed things. Mellowed him out and allowed him to relax after the end of the day. Having a home was a vital component to him and sounded like Shanée leaned the same way.

"I understand. What about now? Do you feel like you're home?"

"I'm getting there."

"Good." He wanted to smile at her, but the dark interior of her car would make the effort futile. "Sorry for interrupting about the fun day incident. Please continue."

"Okay. Well, we went skiing. Everyone came."

"Everyone?"

"Those who weren't mission essential, yes."

"'Kay. Continue."

"So, there I was skiing and actually enjoying myself."

He got the feeling that was rare.

"And I decided to go up to the next slope."

Gabe's gut clenched as he got a sense of where the story was heading. He kept mute, even though his brain formulated a host of questions.

"And a tree came out of nowhere."

He grimaced, then noticed the exit ahead. He flicked on his blinker then exited. As he turned down the next street, Gabe realized Shanée had stopped talking. He listened for silent tears but heard nothing. He spoke softly. "Then what?"

"I tried to stop, tried to swerve out of the way, but I couldn't. My back slammed against the tree, and I passed out."

"I'm so sorry."

"It was a difficult time. I was in physical therapy after surgery and then the military decided I could no longer perform my duties."

"Why is that? I don't mean to be rude or anything, just not sure how they work."

"No, it's a valid question. I had a desk job, and my doctors were saying it wasn't good for me to sit so long."

"What about at Cornwall & Lewis?" Because if Gabe sat around all day—with the occasional breaks for lunch or taking the time to speak to other employees when needed—he could only imagine how much Shanée remained at her desk.

"Mr. Lewis ordered me a special chair. I'm also allowed to take a certain number of days for rest if it comes to that. Plus, he made sure to let me know whatever chairs or footrests, whatever I need, he'll order for me."

"I do notice you walk from time to time."

"It's to keep from stiffening up. I also have a heating pad just for work."

He couldn't imagine having his life altered like that. "How long ago did this happen?"

"Last Christmas."

His breath hitched. In a year her life had been turned upside down. And at Christmas? He didn't even know what to say. No wonder she looked disgruntled whenever a Christmas song came on the speakers—which at Cornwall & Lewis was every song.

"I'm so sorry, Shanée."

A bitter laugh filled the interior, raising the hairs on the back of his neck.

"No reason to apologize. It only confirms what I've known all along." She pointed to a small gray townhome at the end of street. "That's me."

Gabe parked and rushed around the car to open Shanée's door and assist her. She moved gingerly as if afraid to upset the balance she'd created. Or maybe she was in more pain than she'd let on. As they walked up the sidewalk to her front door, Gabe continued the conversation they'd started in the car.

"What is it that you've known all along?"

She blinked, her eyes going wide behind her gold-framed glasses. "That God doesn't care about me."

Shanée's face heated with the admission. She wasn't sure exactly why she was embarrassed, but she was. Maybe because she'd just word vomited on the coworker that had it all together. Gabe held a high position at the bank, owned a home he'd renovated on his own, and belonged to a family that probably kept him baggage free. Admitting that God didn't care for her to a person who probably believed the opposite was more than taboo.

Taking that pain pill on the way home must have loosened her lips.

She unlocked the front door and continued the small steps that had seen her from the car to the house. No way she wanted to risk taking a larger stride and provoking a spasm to rule all spasms. Slowly she turned around to face Gabe. "Thanks for the ride."

His brow dipped. "Will you let me come in and help you? I can make sure you don't fall or anything."

Her heart warmed at the thought, but she threw up a wall before going down the path of *what ifs*. "No. I'm fine now that I'm home." Or she would be soon.

"I'd like to argue that sentiment, but I get what you mean." He stepped back, sliding his hands into his pockets. "Please call me if you need anything. Anything at all."

Shanée nodded then stopped as the movement triggered a spasm. Her jaw clenched as she hissed out a breath of pain.

"Shanée?"

"I'm fine," she croaked.

"You're not." He pulled out his cell phone, fingers flying across the screen. "It says here a stretch can often stop a muscle spasm."

"No," she gritted. "Please no." If she stretched mid-spasm the pain would rival a Charley horse.

"Okay, the second option is massage."

Her face heated. She would *not* let Gabriel Lewis touch her in any way that made her wish fairy tales came true. "That's out as well."

"Might as well be since I'm not a licensed professional. Next suggestion is ice or heat." He looked at her expectantly. "Where's your heating pad?"

Shanée let out a breath as the spasm eased. "On my recliner."

Gabe came forward, gently clasping his hand around hers. "Let's get you settled. And maybe you can tell me why you think God doesn't care about you."

"Hello, Exhibit A." She motioned to her body.

"There were many people in the Bible who suffered ailments."

She stopped, turning her gaze to him. "Like who?" Because she couldn't recall a single person.

"Jacob. In his hip, I believe."

"Jacob?" She knew the name, but her mind felt a little fuzzy as pain threatened to force her into a fetal position.

"You might remember him as Israel."

Her mouth dropped as Gabe guided her into a seated position in the recliner.

He eyed the chair quizzically. "Does this thing have a self-massage option?"

"Yes."

"Good. Turn that on and the heating pad up."

"Boy you're bossy."

He grinned, a look of pure mischief on his face. "I can be."

What did it say about her that the mischievous expression did her in as much as the concerned one?

Shanée clicked the settings for a slight vibration and turned on the heat option. She sighed as tension slowly seeped out of her back. Not tensing up was so hard to do when a spasm hit. The motion only made the pain worse, but her brain seemed to think otherwise.

As sleepiness replaced the pain, Shanée fought to stay awake. "Who else besides Jacob?"

"Paul. One of the apostles asked God to heal him."

"What did He say?" Was her voice trailing? She blinked rapidly, focusing on the scruff on Gabe's face.

"'My grace is sufficient for you, for My strength is made perfect in weakness.'"

She tried not to meet his gaze, but his black eyes were like magnets, locking onto her and refusing to let go. "How is that possible?"

"It's God possible."

Huh? "What do you mean?"

Gabe ran a hand over his face. "Whenever I used to think something was impossible to get done, my mom would always tell me, 'Chin up. It's God possible.'" He gave a sheepish smile. "It was a reminder that I couldn't do it on my own, but *with* God anything was possible."

She had only met Mrs. Lewis for a brief moment at Gabe's birthday party. She sounded like a wise woman, despite the craziness she put out around one holiday.

"What will y'all do next to celebrate?"

Gabe shrugged. "We're trying to decide. Angel wants to go to a tree farm. Something she and Bishop started last year. Starr wants to go to the National Zoo and see the light display they have."

"And Eve? Noel? You?" she asked.

"I honestly don't care as long as I'm with my family. Eve wants to do a tree lighting, and Noel doesn't care either."

Shanée laughed. "It's because y'all are men."

He shook his head. "It's because the venue doesn't matter. As long as we're all together, we're good."

"And your parents? Is Mr. Lewis really going on vacation?" He didn't seem like the type to ever relax.

"Their first time going away since I can remember. They said we're old enough to get together without them leading the charge."

"Hence the party," she said.

"Exactly." This time his grin spelled out mischievousness in all the best ways.

Shanée would have laughed if her brain wasn't in the process of shutting down. "I hope it's epic," she murmured.

"The party will be at their house, so be prepared for pure fun."

"Gabe?"

"Yes?"

"I'm falling asleep." She heard him shift as her eyes had already closed.

"I'll get out of your hair then. Feel better, Shanée."

She sank deeper into the recliner. "Thanks for everything," she mumbled.

Warmth enveloped her, and she vaguely recognized the softness of her chenille throw. "My pleasure," she heard before sleep claimed her.

Chapter Seven

Gabe started the playlist on his cell phone, thankful his car had the Bluetooth option, so he wasn't stuck with the noise on the radio. It was way too early to listen to FM personalities talk and be chipper. He could only handle soft music playing quietly in the background while he drove to work in the dark.

"Can we at least stop for Starbucks?" Gabe asked when he braked at a red light.

Noel shook his head. "Starbucks doesn't open until five."

"Then you should never commute to work before then. It's criminal, I tell you." He glared at his brother.

Noel shrugged. "The light's green." He pointed ahead.

"Because there's no one else driving out here to turn the lights red."

"We were just at a red."

"Fluke," he muttered.

"What's with all that stuff on your face?" Noel asked.

Gabe rubbed a hand down his face. No sleep in his eyes or dried drool remnants on his lips. Wait a minute, he'd washed his face this morning. "What are you talking about?"

Noel laughed. "That black stuff hanging from your chin."

"Hardy har har." *Brothers.* He shook his head. "It was too early to shave. My coffee pot won't even kick on until we're already at work." Plus he thought a beard might look cool in the winter time.

"You'll live."

"Barely," he groused. He couldn't stand Noel's morning person persona. His sickening positivity and zeal for a brand-new day. Unless Gabe had a cup of coffee in hand and a few more hours under his eyelids, he didn't want to be awake.

"There'll be coffee near the bank."

"Yeah, but the café doesn't open until six." Which was still indecent as far as rising hours, but a little better than leaving the house at four in the morning. "If I crash, it's your fault."

"No, it'll be yours because I'm not driving," Noel countered.

Gabe resisted the urge to reach over and shake his brother. "Are you allergic to driving?"

"I did bring your car home."

True, but Gabe was too irritated to concede the point.

They drove a few minutes more in silence, then Noel cleared his throat. Gabe gripped the steering wheel at that particular sound. That noise meant big brother Noel had put his *I'm the oldest and know better* pants on. For whatever reason, Noel wanted to lecture Gabe.

But he refused to make it easy for Noel. He kept driving as if nothing was amiss.

"Ahem," Noel cleared his throat again.

"There's a bottle of water in the back seat if you need something to drink." Gabe maintained a neutral façade though he'd exploded in mental laughter. It may be too early to function but never too early to be a pest to Noel.

"Are we going to talk about the elephant?"

"Sure. It's gray, doesn't actually exist, and now we can move on to your next subject." Gabe bit the inside of his cheek. Who knew the trick to waking up was hassling his big brother?

Noel huffed. "How's Shanée?"

This was about their coworker? "She was sleeping when I left."

"How'd you lock up?"

"Took her house key off the key ring, locked the door, then slipped it through the mail slot."

Noel groaned. "She needs to secure that."

"No one can stick their hand in there." He'd tried, fearing the same thing Noel suggested—that it was unsecure. Unless someone had hired a child to break in, Shanée was safe.

"But apparently they can drop keys and who knows what else in there."

Gabe had thought the same thing, but at least he hadn't left her house unlocked.

"What's going on between you two?" Noel asked.

"Where's this coming from?" Gabe exited the toll road. If he'd known he'd get the third degree, he would have taken an Uber to work and dealt with the expense.

"I saw the way you watched her at dinner then kicked on the hero powers when she didn't feel well."

Gabe's face flushed. "I was just being friendly."

"Okay, but to what end?"

"To be friends, Noel." *Man!* Older brothers were annoying.

"And that's it? You don't want anything more?"

Gabe thought about the question. Did he? He hadn't really considered the idea in detail. Just operating on a feeling here, a hunch there. And now that he'd heard her story, saw the vulnerability behind the tough exterior she presented, Gabe was even more curious. "I'm not sure." But if he was, would he tell Noel?

"At least you're honest."

"Thanks, Noel," he said with full-out sarcasm. He tapped the steering wheel as he drove through D.C. A few people were out driving but otherwise, the city slept. "Can I ask you a question?"

"Of course."

"How do you show a person that God cares about them when they don't believe it?" Gabe had a feeling Shanée hadn't been strictly talking about her health when she'd mentioned *Exhibit A.*

Which had him wondering what other issues in her past contributed to that belief.

"You can't be someone's savior, Gabe."

"I'm not trying to be, *Noel*." He rolled his eyes. "I simply want to be a friend." He shrugged, but his insides felt anything but casual. Because even though he said *friend* his mind balked at the idea. Not that he would examine his feelings.

He was more concerned about Shanée's salvation. Was she saved? Backslidden? Simply angry? Though none of those answers really mattered as much as showing Shanée that God cared. Knowing she'd be at Cornwall & Lewis in a few hours made him a tad eager to get to work, despite the horrendous time of day. Until then, he needed to think of ways he could show her he was trustworthy. But more than that, he wanted her to see God's love.

"Honestly, being a friend reveals God in many ways. Jesus called us friend, so when you become that to someone who maybe has trouble developing friendships, you're showing them that God cares. What you should be praying for, in my opinion, is that she sees God in everyday actions. It's that disconnect that has people believing He isn't concerned with their lives. Pray her eyes are opened."

Gabe glanced at Noel. "That's actually pretty insightful."

Noel huffed. "Bruh, I've got more than one thought in my brain."

"You mean besides loans and how Cornwall & Lewis runs?"

"Exactly."

Gabe held back a laugh. "When will you start dating seriously?" *Let's put the shoe on the other foot.* See how Noel appreciated being interrogated over his lack of a love life.

"I don't have time." Noel shifted in his seat. "Besides, where would I meet a good woman? In the bank?"

"Stranger things have happened." He'd met Shanée in the bank.

"Who knows. Maybe I'll stay single."

"Really?" Gabe parked the car and stared at his brother. "You don't want to marry? Have a family? Build a life similar to Mom and Dad?" Because he thought they'd had it perfect growing up.

Noel rubbed the back of his neck. "I don't know. I mean, I used to think I would have a family and whatnot. But Gabe, I'm thirty-five. If it hasn't happened by now . . ."

"It could still happen."

"Maybe, but I'm not going to stress about it."

Good point. They got out of the car, a nip of wind making Gabe thankful he had a wool cap on.

"Are you contemplating marriage, little brother?"

Gabe resisted the urge to roll his eyes at the moniker. Being in the middle had its advantages, but it also sucked when it came to talking to Noel and Eve. They always liked to remind him he was younger.

"Thinking of life in general." The marriage thing was something he'd only thought about when talking to God. He wasn't ready to share his feelings with Noel.

Noel stopped at the front door, brow in a V. "You don't like working here, do you?"

He blew out a breath. Should have known Noel would dive right into the heart of things. He really had an uncanny knack for weeding out people's issues.

Gabe huffed. "I'm good with numbers. I don't *mind* working here, but sometimes I wonder if there could be more."

"More what?"

That's exactly what Gabe wanted to know. Instead of voicing that, he shrugged and walked in behind Noel. Bonding time was over. Time for each man to go to their separate corners. Where Gabe would take the opportunity and wonder how he could help Shanée.

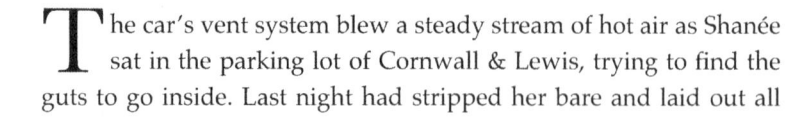

The car's vent system blew a steady stream of hot air as Shanée sat in the parking lot of Cornwall & Lewis, trying to find the guts to go inside. Last night had stripped her bare and laid out all her insecurities before Gabe. He'd seen her back rebel against her healthcare regimen, had dragged out the details of her accident, and had probably seen her fall asleep.

Lord willing, he hadn't seen her drool or anything else unsightly.

Despite those unnerving truths, she'd slept peacefully, waking up to a back that had returned to *its* normal. Not that her spine and nerves would revert to pre-accident condition, but it was down to an annoying pain versus tear-inducing.

And she had Gabe's assistance to thank for that.

But how could she walk inside the bank doors, thank Gabe for last night, and still maintain her dignity? As it was, her pride lay in tatters and her insecurity had ratcheted up to force protection Delta levels. Her body armored up, ready to attack the highest threats coming her way—and Gabe was on all the wanted posters.

Still, she had to thank him. Which was why she'd taken a detour to buy him coffee. She'd stopped at the café near the bank, thankful the barista knew exactly who Shanée referred to when trying to get his exact order. Now she had a medium dark roast with a shot of espresso, a dash of milk, and two sugar packets. Shanée had experienced a pang of irritation when the woman had enthusiastically recalled Gabe's order without fail. Something told her she wasn't that good at her job and the memory had everything to do with the handsome man who exuded holiday cheer and the Christmas spirit.

"Get out of the car, Mitchell. You can't thank him hiding in here." True, but she also didn't have to worry about the pitying glances he'd send her way. "He won't appreciate cold coffee."

Still, she couldn't move. Did she really have to tell him she thought God had forgotten about her? If she was still a praying woman, she'd ask God for relief from this embarrassment. Instead, she straightened her shoulders and opened the door. The wind nipped at her face, shredded its way through her coat threads, and slapped against her skin. Wasn't a thick jacket supposed to protect against the elements? She would have done better with a military-issued weather coat.

She pushed against the wind and sighed in relief when the bank doors closed behind her, ushering her into the warmth. The forecast had predicted an Artic chill, with gusts dropping the wind chill to below zero, but Shanée had thought the weatherman told a joke. Surely D.C. didn't get that kind of cold. There weren't mountains out here. Then again, the Atlantic harbor could be found a few miles —and hours of traffic—away.

Walking past the front and into the back, Shanée kept her head down until she entered her office. She placed her briefcase down and laid her jacket on the back of her chair. A quick glance at the wall clock let her know Gabe would already be working. All she had to do was march in there, hand him the coffee, and say *thank you* before making a quick exit. Satisfied with the plan, she grabbed the to-go mug and left her office.

She rapped on Gabe's doorjamb and inhaled a deep breath.

"Come in."

Shanée crossed the threshold. "Morning." Why was her mouth so dry?

"Shanée." Gabe beamed, pleasure exuding from him like heat waves. "How you feeling this morning?"

She thrust the coffee cup in his face. "This is for you. A thank you for last night." Her face heated. That sounded intimate and not at *all* what she'd meant. "I mean for helping. Uh, yeah, thank you."

A bemused expression curved his lips and had lines popping around his eyes in amusement. "My pleasure."

"Really?" She scoffed. "Watching after a grown woman because she had a little bit of back pain?"

"Don't." He held up a hand. "Please don't belittle your pain," he said softly.

She froze, unsure of what to say or how to process his comment. Because if she didn't belittle her pain as Gabe put it, then she'd have to come to grips with never being the same again. To accept that she truly wouldn't get any better. That on the days it was unbearable, tears were her only companion. But acknowledging those feelings threatened her precarious hold on control.

Stuffing her emotions to the farthest corner in the recesses of her mind was the only way she'd made it this far. If she didn't poke fun at her injury, then her jokes would quickly turn into sobs. Shanée licked her lips and gave a quick nod, hiding all her thoughts behind a mask of nonchalance.

"Well, thank you again."

"Of course. You're feeling better today? Found your key?"

"Much." She swallowed. "And yes. Thank you for locking up."

"No problem. But you really should seal up that mail slot."

She rolled her eyes. It was the first thing her dad had said when she'd sent pictures of the place. "I'll put that on my to-do list."

He laughed. "I have a feeling that just went in one ear and flew out the other."

"Maybe it didn't fly."

"Oh, it did," he crossed his arms and took a sip of his drink. An inscrutable expression filtered across his face.

Had they messed up his order? "What's wrong?" she asked.

"The coffee . . ." He stared at the cardboard container.

"Did they make a mistake?" Guess the barista mistook Gabe for someone else.

"No. This is exactly how I order it." He studied her. "How did you know?"

"The barista. I described you and she rattled off your order, so I asked her to make it."

"You asked about *me?*"

Why was he looking at her like that? Had she done something wrong? "You drove me home and left the event with your brothers and sisters early. *For me.* The least I could do was figure out what kind of drink you like. After all, you're always buying coffee for others."

"I appreciate this." He held the cup up. "I really do."

"Good." She took a step back. "I'll let you get back to work."

He cocked his head to the side. "Want to do lunch?"

Yes! No. *Ugh.* "Um, I have a lot of work to do today."

"But you have to eat, right?"

She did, and maybe if she bought him lunch, she could call them even. "All right. Lunch."

He beamed. "Fantastic. One o'clock?"

"I'll be ready."

But she had a feeling she'd never be ready to analyze the feelings Gabe awakened in her.

Chapter Eight

The GPS announced the arrival to his destination, and Gabe put the car in park right as Shanée's front door opened. He hurried around the passenger side to open the door for her. Yesterday Shanée had agreed to come with him and his family to a tree farm in Winchester, Virginia.

Gabe had already checked to see how much walking they'd be doing because he didn't want to cause Shanée any more pain. Fortunately, the owner was really accommodating and helped Gabe come up with a plan. With the owner's assurance, Shanée said yes to another event. That, and he liked to think his charm over lunch the other day had worked in his favor.

He motioned for her to enter as she walked toward him. "Your carriage awaits."

She chuckled, then eyed his vehicle warily.

"Is there a problem?" His stomach twisted. Had he messed up already?

"Uh, your car is kind of low to the ground."

He studied the sleek sedan. It was a little low, but it also had a sunroof and a nice kick of acceleration when he wanted to speed on the toll roads. He never took into account that lowering oneself to sit could be a chore, but now . . .

"I'm an idiot."

Shanée shook her head. "You're not, but you don't have to worry about ailments either."

"But I thought I'd considered everything," he groaned.

"It's not the end of the world. We can take my car." She pointed to a crossover in the driveway.

In the broad daylight, it looked like a roller skate. If he hadn't already driven it, he'd wonder how he'd ever fit. *Good thing life's not about you.* This was about Shanée and being a friend, for now.

"All right. Is it okay if I leave my car in your driveway?"

"Of course."

Gabe rounded the front of the car, kicking himself mentally all the way. Of course she didn't want to lower herself into his almost sports sedan. He slid into the driver's seat. Maybe he should trade in his vehicle. *Whoa.* Where had that thought come from? It's not like they were dating or even in a serious relationship.

His hands gripped the wheel as he waited for her to reverse and allow him the space to park in the driveway. All the time his mind tripped over his thoughts.

Why not ask her out?

Just be her friend right now.

No, let her know you're interested in more.

Every thought seemed like a bad idea. Asking her out would be awful if she had absolutely no interest in him that way. Just being her friend felt restrictive, as if he'd land himself in the friend zone with no way to alert her that he wanted more. And telling her he wanted more but leaving the ball in her court felt worse than asking her on a date.

What do I do, Lord? Help me out, please!

He placed his scarf around his neck then shrugged into the peacoat. He left the jacket unbuttoned as he grabbed his beanie, wallet, and car keys. His cell was already in his coat pocket, so Gabe didn't have to worry about that. After locking up his vehicle, he trotted over to Shanée's hatchback idling at the curb.

Warmth greeted the seat of his pants as hot air blew on his face. "Wow, never thought one of these cars would have heated seats."

"It's a must."

He buckled and held up his cell. "I have directions or . . ." He pointed to her nav. "Do you want me to input the address?"

"You can give me directions. Be my navigator." She grinned at him.

His pulse picked up speed. She had a beautiful smile. "All right then. Toll roads or no toll roads?"

She mock-shuddered. "No toll roads. I like taking back streets."

Interesting. He always liked to get from point A to point B as quickly as possible. "Why do you like taking the long way?"

"I'm not in a hurry, and even when I need to get to work, if I leave at a decent enough hour, I'll still arrive on time."

"The things you learn about a person."

"You're a toll road guy?"

"The faster the better."

"Doesn't that leave you all stressed though?"

He paused before spouting an immediate no. "Not at all. Driving itself relaxes me. When I have to slow down is when I get antsy."

"How many speeding tickets do you have?"

He laughed. "You'll notice I avoided buying a red car."

"It still looks like a sporty vehicle."

True, but most police officers would recognize that his wasn't. Besides, if a person drove with the flow of traffic, avoiding a ticket became that much easier. Fortunately, many D.C. metro drivers preferred speeds over seventy miles per hour. *Win win.*

"Since we're going to the tree farm, does that mean the zoo is out?"

Gabe shook his head. "No, we decided to do that tomorrow. You're more than welcome to join us, but if you've never been to the Zoo, let me warn you now."

"Uh oh. What's wrong with it?"

"Lots of hills." He studied her. "I figured those would be a problem. That's the only reason I didn't invite you." Because he'd wanted to ask her. The thought of hanging out with her all weekend made him happier than an open highway and an eighty-miles-per-hour speed limit sign.

"That sounds like a muscle-relaxer-heating-pad kind of night."

He grimaced. "May I ask a question?" He peeked at her.

She'd worn her glasses today, and her hair fell in loose waves, a knitted cap slouching towards the crown of her head. She looked adorable, and Gabe was overcome with the need to protect her.

"Sure. Go for it. But I reserve the right to leave it unanswered."

"Fair enough." He paused, gathering his thoughts. "How much of your daily life is limited to the status of how your back feels?"

A quiet sigh escaped her lips. "Too much it seems. I'm just not at the point where I think it's smart to press through the pain without suffering the consequences."

He'd never thought about pressing through the pain. Were there people who did that? How many people suffered from chronic issues? How many were limited to what their bodies said felt good or not? He'd always had good health, and right then, felt a little selfish for taking it for granted.

"I'm sorry you have to even look through that lens."

"It's difficult. I was extremely bitter after the accident. *Extremely.*"

"And now?"

This time, she paused. "Honestly?"

"Please. If you feel comfortable enough to share, that is." And he prayed she did.

"I'm still bitter. I still have *why me* moments. I don't understand why healing isn't mine. Why I still have to deal with this a year after the accident."

Gabe felt woefully inadequate for this conversation. Life had been easy for him, and he had no wisdom on what to say. What would Jesus say? What would He do? *Lord, help!*

"I prayed and prayed and prayed, and nothing. My mom and dad prayed and received the same results. The military chaplain came and prayed." She huffed. "I've been prayed over so many times, it would be laughable if it didn't shed light on a darker truth."

His heart sank, knowing exactly what she'd say.

"God simply doesn't care about me. How could He if so many people prayed and the answer was no to all?"

Gabe's mind emptied as he prayed for wisdom and for God to use him to get Shanée's attention. Because God *did* care, and she needed to see that.

Silence descended between them, and Shanée wanted to shrink into her seat, knowing she was the reason for the awkwardness. But Gabe had asked, and he deserved the truth. God didn't care about her. Why else would He have allowed her to continue to be in pain?

"I can't begin to explain how wrong you are."

She startled at the sound of Gabe's smooth voice. It was like honey on a biscuit and had the power to lull her to sleep or awaken every nerve ending not attuned to pain. *Wait, focus.* She cleared her throat. "How can you say that? I'm still in pain."

"That, I cannot discount. But let me ask you this—have you ever done something you regret? Something bad?"

Her face heated. "Perhaps."

"You're thinking of it right now, aren't you?"

She nodded, refusing to look over his way. He didn't know her thoughts ran to her first boyfriend and the mistakes she couldn't undo.

"Okay. Keep that in mind. I'm not going to ask what it is, but I am going to make some assumptions. Correct me if I get them wrong, all right?"

"O-kay." She didn't know where he was going, but she'd humor him.

"You regret this incident, right?"

"I do." That was easy enough to answer.

"If you could go back in time, you'd avoid it. Right?"

In a heartbeat. "Yes." She regretted caving in, but more than that she wished she'd never even said yes when he asked her out.

"I'm assuming this incident would fall on the sin scale."

Shanée blinked, surprised by his comment. "Yep," she muttered.

"Good."

"What?"

Gabe laughed. "Stick with me. I promise it'll make sense in a little bit."

"Right," she drawled.

"Prior to the accident, would you consider yourself a Christian? A believer?"

"Yes. I went to church." Grew up in it actually. Had even committed her life to Christ in Sunday school when she was eight.

"So, you know all about salvation?"

"I do."

"Okay. Pretend you're near death and you've come to stand before God."

Her heart started pounding. "I'm pretending."

"God gives you a choice. He asks you if you'd rather be healed and returned to earth to live out the remainder of your days."

His voice trailed off, and Shanée's breath hitched. "Or?" she asked softly.

"Or have your sins wiped off your slate. You'll return back to live the rest of your days until He calls you home, but you'll never have to worry about any regrets or mistakes because He'll always forgive them."

Her eyes watered as she stared out the windshield. Her heart knew the answer, but her head wanted to argue. To ask for both.

"What do you choose?" Gabe murmured.

Shanée thought of the shame she'd felt after dating her first boyfriend. How she ignored the male gender for the next few years after. Eventually, she'd dated again, but she could never get close to anyone. Whether that was self-preservation kicking in or the guys realizing they couldn't take the relationship to another level without a marriage certificate, she didn't know. Never thought too deeply for fear she'd fall apart.

"I'd choose forgiveness," she replied.

"There's a verse in the Bible that says 'my grace is sufficient for you'. God chooses to forgive all who believe in His Son and recognize their need of a Savior. Who understand their sins prevent them from communing with God." Gabe laid a hand on her arm and squeezed lightly. "I can't answer as to why He heals some and doesn't heal others. But I know that your pain, your suffering, doesn't disqualify you from His love and goodness. He still has wonderful plans for you. He still has a purpose for you."

"But if I only get to choose between forgiveness and healing, His forgiveness is enough." She sighed, understanding coursing through her.

"More than enough. His grace has no limits, Shanée."

A tear trailed down her cheek. "Thank you, Gabe. Thank you for putting it so plainly but not patronizing me."

"It's my pleasure. Maybe you'd like to go with me to church Sunday?"

"You're not tired of me yet?" She joked, hoping levity would lighten the atmosphere. She hadn't expected a heavy conversation when he'd invited her out.

"I'm pretty sure that couldn't happen."

Her cheeks heated, and she clamped her teeth over her tongue to keep from smiling. Somehow Gabe was slowly wheedling his way into her heart.

The rest of their conversation remained light and superficial as she made her way to Winchester. Soon she pulled into a parking space in front of the tree farm. She waved at Gabe's sister in the car next to them.

"I can't believe we arrived at the same time," she remarked.

"Me either. Angel is always saying how Marvel delays them as they get ready."

"That's her stepdaughter, right?"

"Yep. She's a pistol."

They got out of the car, and Shanée greeted the Lewis siblings. Noel, Eve, Angel, Starr, and their significant others were all bundled and ready to cut down a tree.

"Do you have a tree already?" Shanée asked Gabe.

"I do. Do you?"

She shook her head. "No. I've never decorated before."

He raised an eyebrow. "Never ever?"

"We didn't have a lot growing up so Christmas became one of those holidays we avoided."

"Oh, we're fixing that today."

She laughed. "I don't think I can get a tree back to my home." She pointed to the hatchback. "I don't own a truck."

"Sure you can. We'll get it tied to the roof of your car. They'll know what to do. But first," he held out the crook of his elbow. "I have something else planned for you."

"You do?"

He nodded, a sly grin on his face.

What was he up to?

Gabe waved to Eve. "We'll catch up in about ten minutes."

"You sure?"

"Positive."

Obviously, Gabe knew something the rest of them didn't. She let him lead her away from the crowd and right up to an empty field. "What are we doing here?"

"Waiting for your ride."

"What?" She stopped as the sound of sleigh bells reached them. A barn door opened, and a horse and carriage came out.

"Are we—?" She couldn't even finish her question.

"We are. I made arrangements for them to take us to the area where they chop down trees. Didn't want you to have to walk up hills or anything. He also guaranteed warm blankets and lumbar support."

Her eyes welled up. "Gabe . . ."

"I'm great, aren't I?" He winked.

She laughed through the tears. "You might be perfect." She rose up slowly on her toes and laid a kiss on his cheek.

What was meant to be quick turned into a lingering touch. She pulled back, meeting his warm gaze.

His eyes flickered down to her lips then back up. "You'd try the patience of a saint."

"Or an angel," she murmured.

His head fell back, laughter filling the air as the sleigh bells rang louder.

Right in that moment, with the conversation in the car and careful planning Gabe had shown her, Shanée began to wonder if she'd been wrong about God all along.

Chapter Nine

Nervousness was a ridiculous emotion to feel when picking someone up for church, but Gabe had quickly learned Shanée wasn't just any someone. He couldn't help but believe this visit mattered. Shanée seemed to have cut off communication with God, and he was hopeful enough that bringing her to church would open the gateway once more. Though a teeny tiny part of him worried she would continue to freeze the Lord out.

Gabe grabbed his wallet and keys and headed out before he could worry more about whether or not Shanée would like his church. At least he didn't have to worry about his clothes. The sweater vest would keep him warm and look respectable at the same time. Not that his church was big on what a person wore. He'd seen men in suits and others in cargo shorts—well, in the summertime at least.

He still couldn't believe she'd agreed to come today. She also said she'd come back to his place for lunch. Yesterday, he'd passed the extra set of keys to Noel and Eve who were in charge of the afternoon meal. Starr and Angel had other plans and wouldn't be able to make it. Gabe needed to grab a pie or something fitting for dessert.

Probably pie because he'd always choose *pie*. Apple, to be more specific, with ice cream on top. His stomach rumbled in appreciation, and he detoured into the nearest grocery store. If they didn't have his favorite sweet, he'd have to figure something else out.

After grabbing two pies, Gabe drove straight to Shanée's house. He'd borrowed Noel's SUV so that Shanée could relax as a passenger. He told her to bring a lumbar pillow and anything else she'd need to be comfortable. This morning, he'd texted her to remind her to bring extra pain meds just in case.

Since Shanée had opened up about her accident, Gabe started doing research after work, doing all he could to learn about her troubles. He'd been tempted to add a supportive recliner, heating pad, and self-massagers to his Amazon cart and have them all shipped to his home. But knowing he'd intended them for his own home and not hers had made him pause.

What was he doing?

He was going half-crazy over a woman he barely knew. Though he wanted to know everything about her. That had to count for something, right? He sighed and got out of the car, pulling his unbuttoned peacoat closer with his hands in the pockets to block out the chill. No point in closing the jacket when he'd take it right off again once he got in the car. The heat blasting from the vents kept him from needing the garment.

He knocked on the door and waited. Shanée opened the door, a wobbly smile on her face. She looked great in a cranberry-colored sweater that matched her lipstick.

"Morning." He grinned, hoping to coax a bigger smile from her and erase any nerves she was experiencing.

"Morning, Gabe. Let me grab my coat and Bible, okay?"

"Sure."

"You can come in," she yelled over her shoulder as she strode away.

He stood in the foyer, shutting the door to keep the heat from escaping. He could practically hear his mom's voice in the back of his head yelling about letting the hot air out. The sound of shoes squeaking against the wood floors broke through his woolgathering.

Shanée held a Bible in one of those quilted cases in one hand and a black wool coat that fell to her shins in the other. "I'm ready."

"Great. Let me help you with your coat first."

"Thank you."

She handed the garment to him and he held it open as she slipped her arms into the sleeves. He lifted her soft hair from inside the coat. His fingers wanted to pause, draw her closer. Instead, he cleared his throat and took a step back.

She locked up, then he guided her down the frozen drive.

"Wow. I didn't realize it was this icy out."

"Yeah. The side roads are pretty bad, but the highway has already been taken care of." Thank goodness, because sliding into a ditch wasn't a good start to the expectations he had for today.

"Why didn't they do the side roads?" She looked at him quizzically.

"It's northern Virginia." He shrugged. "I'm convinced that they never take the forecast seriously when needed and always overreact when not."

Shanée shook her head as she got in the car and he followed suit, directing the car toward his church. It was a good thing she lived in northern Virginia and not in D.C. Sometimes he'd drive down and go to church with his family, but more often than not, he stayed near his house. No need to commute on the weekend as well.

"I'm guessing your church is pretty standard?" she asked. "Music, sermon, and that's it?"

"It is, but today they said there would be special music." Though he couldn't remember the specifics.

"What does that mean?"

"No clue." He shot her a sheepish look before gazing back at the road. "I missed that information. I don't know if they sent it in an email or said it when I was thinking of something else."

She laughed. "You weren't playing on your phone in church, were you?"

"Nope. I'll open the Bible app on my phone, but I always cease notifications during that time so that I won't be distracted."

Soon Gabe pulled into the church parking lot and hurried to open Shanée's door. *Lord, please let her connect with the worship, with Your word, and anything else You have planned for her.* Because as much as he wanted her reconciled with God, he knew this wasn't about him. Her anger at God was about Shanée's relationship with the Lord. Gabe simply needed to hold that thought in the forefront of his mind so he wouldn't make it all about him.

At least, I'll try not to, Lord.

Greeters smiled at the doors, holding them open and allowing them to pass through.

"Morning, Gabe."

"Morning, Arnold," Gabe replied, shaking the older gentleman's hand.

"I see you brought a guest."

"I did. Meet Shanée. Shanée, this is Arnold, best greeter in the state of Virginia."

"Ha." The older man shook his head. "I'm just the oldest."

"Are you really?" she asked.

Arnold laughed, shaking a wizened finger in Gabe's direction. "I might as well be, but I'm only the oldest here."

"And he's not saying how old that is exactly," Gabe interjected.

"One day someone will get it right and I'll admit it."

Gabe shook his head, a chuckle escaping at the merriment the old man had at the congregation's expense. He never admitted how old he was, and Gabe told Shanée as much as he directed her to the refreshment table.

"Want some juice? I hear it's caffeine free."

She huffed out a small laugh. "I'm fine. I had breakfast at home."

He exaggerated a wide-eyed stare. "What'd you do that for? That's why we have a refreshment table." He grabbed a bear claw. "No need to waste your own food."

"Aren't we eating at your house after church?"

"Yeah, but by the time we get back, it'll be almost two hours since this bear claw."

"You poor overgrown boy."

You can make fun of me anytime. Because if it lit up Shanée's pretty brown eyes like they were now, then he would gladly play the fool. He took a huge bite of the pastry and closed his eyes, listening to her laughter.

After finishing his food and grabbing a cup of coffee—because you could never have too many—he led the way into the sanctuary. Immediately his soul perked up, faster than the caffeine's effect. There was something about walking into the church that seemed to peel away the stress.

That, and the worship team picked the best songs. Gabe waved to folks, introduced Shanée to a few more, then settled into chairs midway through the sanctuary.

"Is this spot okay?" he asked, whispering in her ear.

She nodded, placing a pillow behind her back.

He clamped his mouth shut on the second question echoing in his mind as the sound of cymbals rippling across the room grabbed his attention. It was time to worship and pray that God would heal her hurts. He dropped his head, opened his heart, and prayed.

Almost a year had passed since Shanée had stepped foot in a church. She hated that she was braced for disappointment. From the moment Gabe knocked on her door, her insides had been heaving up and down along with the roller coaster of emotions she felt. She wanted to connect to God, to believe He cared, but she couldn't forget the many months where she heard nothing.

A year of feeling forgotten.

Twelve months of constant pain.

365 days of *why me* without an answer in sight.

She let the music wash over her, feeling a prick of remembrance as the words lauded God and how good He was. But was He?

That was the one thing she just couldn't reconcile. How could a good God let something like this happen to her? How could He think that being in pain twenty-four-seven with no break was good for her? How could He stand by and watch as she begged for healing until she finally realized that He either didn't care or wouldn't because this was some part of His "good" plan?

There was nothing good about pain.

Nothing good about suffering.

She was tired of feeling tired. Of being tired of the pain. Okay, so she had to say that last thought two times. But seriously, how could the worship team sing about God's goodness? Didn't they have something in their life they were suffering from? She wasn't the only person who had health issues. One stop at the Veteran's Hospital in D.C. proved that. And even in that location, she heard vets say they were blessed because it was another day above ground.

She just couldn't understand the sentiment.

But she wanted to. If she could even feel that spark of hope like she used to, trust in God's goodness like she used to, maybe this darkness would leave her. Maybe she could survive this Christmas. She glanced at the man beside her.

His head had been bowed since the music started. Was this how he worshipped? Was he praying? She couldn't help but feel like Gabe was a personal hug from God. A memento that He hadn't forgotten her. Yet she couldn't just wipe a year's worth of pain and believing He had abandoned little Nay Nay Mitchell, as people back home used to call her.

She closed her eyes. *Do You still think about me? Do You care?*

Goosebumps broke across her arms as a very real answer spoke in her spirit. It wasn't an audible *yes*, but it might as well have been the way her soul felt instant comfort. Tears sprang to her eyes, threatening to breach the seal of her lashes as she kept them shut.

"Lord," she whispered questioningly as the singers continued into a new song. There was no answer, but that comforting feeling didn't dissipate.

The sensation remained throughout the sermon and as she and Gabe exited the building. The sun shone brightly despite the frigid temperatures that had her huddling within her coat. As Gabe slowly made his way out of the busy parking lot, Shanée reflected over the last hour and a half.

"What did you think?" Gabe asked.

"You have a nice church." That was evident by the people welcoming newcomers, greeting old friends, and chatting with anyone who walked by.

"What did you think of the sermon?"

She paused to search for the words. The preacher's topic had obviously been well researched. His impassioned plea at the end for people to turn to God sounded authentic and real. But Shanée was stuck with unanswered questions.

Don't forget God's presence.

Yet how could she even sum it all up to Gabe? "It was a good sermon."

"Just good?"

Was that an edge to his voice or her own nerves twisting the tone and nuances? She turned to study him. "You obviously go to a nice church, Gabe. And it did my heart well to be there." She paused, trying to gather her thoughts. "I'm just not sure how to reconcile the past year with the belief that God is good." She stared at her hands, hoping she hadn't offended the one person who ignored her bluster and dug deep.

A light touch trailed down the back of her hand and hooked around her pinky. She stared at Gabe's much larger finger, curled around her petite one.

"Okay," he whispered.

She let out a small breath. They maintained the contact all the way back to his house where he pulled up into his drive. She took in the red-brick home with cream siding. There was a small front porch and a two-car garage to the left.

"It's beautiful."

"Wait until you see the inside."

She followed him, looping her travel pillow over one arm like a fur muff. If only it were that glamorous instead of the sad tale of a woman who simply couldn't stand to sit in most chairs.

"You did all the work yourself, right?"

"I sure did." He pointed to the bushes lined under a window. "Planted those bushes and the flowers currently taking a winter break around the mailbox."

"Do you have a lawn service?"

He shook his head as he gestured for her to enter the house. "I like to do the yard work." He hung up their coats then clapped his hands together. "Want a tour?"

"Please."

It was easy to catch Gabe's vision as he talked about restoring the floors, painting the walls, and even knocking a couple of them down. The doorway leading to the dining area held a lovely arch he'd widened to give a more open feel but still maintain the cozy cut-off vibe to the dining room.

His words, not hers.

There seemed to be an extra sparkle in his eyes as he described all that he had done in each room. Shanée stopped him as they entered the hall, headed back toward the kitchen where half of his family waited.

"How come you don't do this for a living?"

"What?" His brow quizzed. "Restore homes?"

"Yes. It's obvious you love it."

"Well, yeah. I love working with my hands, but crunching numbers pays the bills." He stared at her as if she should understand.

But she didn't. She genuinely loved numbers, finances, and finding errors most people couldn't. She'd never seen Gabe have this much passion at work. Which was probably a good thing because he was practically infectious at this point. She just wanted to wrap him in a hug, squeeze, and never let go.

She swallowed, returning her thoughts to the subject at hand. "Why couldn't this pay the bills? How much equity do you have now?"

He lifted a shoulder as if it never occurred to him, but the next number out of his mouth proved otherwise.

She let out a low breath. "Now imagine if you sold this home. You'd immediately make a profit."

"Yeah, but I'm no house flipper. I just wanted a comfortable place to come and lay my head. Maybe have guests over from time to time. And someday in the future, raise a family. I'm not trying to earn back the amount I spent in it right away."

"No, but that doesn't mean you couldn't have a profitable business doing so." Could she get him to backtrack on that family subject?

Of course not. You're not family material. What do you have to offer him?

"Not everyone is the next HGTV star."

She chuckled. "I know that, but I also know you don't come alive talking about numbers like you do this restoration." She hooked her pinky in his, squeezed, then let go. "Think about it."

"All right," he murmured, his eyes darkening from the touch.

She walked away before her heart could convince her that a kiss between them would make everything better.

Because even *if* he had looked at her with desire in his eyes, Shanée wasn't ready to trust another man with her weary heart. Not to mention saddling someone with her high maintenance life.

But what about in sickness or health?

She rolled her eyes. Those were for people already married, *not* potential dates. How would it sound for her to say *Hi, I'm Shanée Mitchell and I suffer from chronic pain. Want to go out? Oh wait, but not that place because sitting in those chairs makes me want to crawl out of my skin. Wait, not there either because my legs don't reach the floor and it makes the neuropathy pain worse.*

Knock it off, Mitchell. She blew out a breath and reached for the fakest smile possible. No need for Eve or Noel to know the battle going on in her head. Especially since the hairs on the back of her neck tingled with an awareness of Gabe's incoming presence. She needed to act like life was wonderful and there was nothing to worry about.

Chapter Ten

Gabe couldn't stop thinking about Shanée's words. Though she probably meant them as encouragement and a compliment to his restoration skills, they rang like accusations and created a host of doubts.

How come you don't do this for a living?
You don't come alive talking about numbers like you do the restoration.
Think about it.

Which was all he'd been doing. When the alarm went off for work this morning, those were the first words in his mind: *think about it*. They'd also been the last words before he'd fallen asleep last night. They were still ringing in his ears as he took care of his grooming needs.

Shanée had managed to create an earworm that made him question every single adult decision he'd ever made. Had he made a mistake going into finance? Would Dad be disappointed if he left Cornwall & Lewis? Would Noel?

He shook his head and flicked off the bathroom light. He headed for the front door where his shoes rested on the rack. Could he seriously restore homes for a living? Walk away from the bank? Something in his spirit shifted. A curiosity and something that felt a little like hope.

Maybe this was the *more* he'd been searching for. Maybe this could be the next step. Was it greedy to ask the Lord for Shanée to also be part of his future plans? Not that he necessarily wanted her to go into business with him. He was more interested in a life partnership, and something told him she was *the one*. Which was ridiculous. They hadn't even gone out on a date yet.

What about going to make chocolate bombs?

That had ended up a disaster since her back had ended up hurting. But prior to that, it had felt like a date. They'd kind of been in their own world at the end of the table while the rest of his siblings had laughed and chattered among themselves. Not that they'd excluded them or anything, Gabe had been too wrapped up in discovering who Shanée was. The way he figured it, he'd already been dating her, just never realized the fact until now.

His lips curved into a smile, then he whistled on the way out the door.

Not even the chilly air could dampen his good mood. The feelings lasted right until he walked into Cornwall & Lewis and found Shanée's office empty.

He set the rooibos tea he'd bought for her on the desk. The lady at the café had assured him the drink was a good alternative to caffeinated tea and one Shanée would like. But she wasn't here. Was she sick?

He pulled his cell out of his pocket. A few clicks here and there and his texts were open with her name front and center.

Gabe: Morning. Are you okay?

Please be okay. Please be okay. Maybe she'd thrown her back out. Though she'd seemed perfectly fine when he'd dropped her off at her place yesterday evening.

Shanée: Good morning. I'm fine. Parents are coming today. Forgot to mention it yesterday because I completely forgot until my alarm woke me this morning to remind me.

Yikes.

Gabe: Are you at the airport now?

Shanée: Yes. Waiting for my parents in baggage claim.

Gabe: Then I'll leave you be.
Shanée: Have a good day.
Gabe: You too.

He stared at his phone, brain whirling with a thousand thoughts. He tapped out another message.

Gabe: Hey, would your parents like to go to the Christmas party too?
Shanée: That's nice of you but not necessary.
Gabe: Well, you are my date, so I think it sounds perfect.

Because they hadn't been on a single outing by themselves, why change things now?

Shanée: If you're sure.
Gabe: I am.
Shanée: Then we'll be there.
Gabe: I'm still picking you up.

She sent a laughing emoji with the word *fine*.

Gabe grinned. Now all he needed was a plan to convince her they were perfect for each other. But first, he needed to talk to Noel. He walked down the hall, distributing coffees to his other coworkers before knocking on his brother's door.

"Come in."

Gabe peeked in, relieved no one else occupied the room. He slipped inside and shut the door behind him.

"Hey, Gabe. Work or personal?" Noel asked, loosening his tie as he sat down.

"Um, both." Gabe sat in the leather chair across from his brother. "But let's go with personal before you put on your work hat."

"Fair enough. What's going on?"

"How big of a deal would it be if I gave notice and quit?"

Noel's eyes bugged out as his jaw dropped.

"Apparently pretty big," Gabe continued as if he hadn't shocked his older brother. "Would Dad have the same reaction?" he asked tentatively. Because as much as he wanted Noel's respect, Dad mattered the most.

"Uh. W-what?" Noel held up a hand. "Start over. I think I missed a few thousand words."

Gabe sighed and ran a hand over his beard. "Shanée asked me why I didn't restore homes for a living. Said I didn't talk about numbers with half the passion I did about the improvements I made in my home."

Noel's brows shot up. "You want to restore homes? For a living? Am I hearing you right?"

Gabe swallowed. "I'm processing right now and part of that is finding out how you two would feel about the change."

"Okay. I can understand gathering information." Noel steepled his hands. "Honestly, if you're not happy here and restoring homes would make you happier, I'd understand the switch. I just don't want you to sink your money into an idea that will cause more stress. You have no guarantee the business would succeed."

"You're right. I don't, but isn't that where faith comes in?"

Noel tilted his head as if conceding the point to Gabe. "I don't think Dad would flip. But if you tell him, tell him the moment he gets back from his vacation. He may still be in a mellow mood by then."

Gabe chuckled. "True."

"Do you have a business plan yet?"

"No. I just now came to the conclusion that the idea held any kind of merit. I'd been fighting against the thought."

"The guaranteed money here versus the unknown, huh?"

"Exactly." Gabe leaned back in the chair, taking a sip of his coffee. "Plus, I really don't want you or Dad upset with me."

"Wow, little brother, I never realized you were such a people pleaser."

"What? No. I'm not."

Noel raised an eyebrow as if to say *are you sure?* And oddly enough, Gabe wasn't. Hadn't he followed Dad's footsteps because the path was easy? He knew Dad would be proud and that the money would practically fall into his lap.

"Maybe I really am."

"My suggestion?"

Gabe nodded.

"Find out what God wants and go from there."

Truer words had never been spoken. Gabe stood and saluted with his coffee cup. "Later, bro."

"Go pray," Noel shouted as Gabe closed his office door.

Already on it.

"This traffic is otherworldly," Mom said.

Shanée smirked. "I told you."

"And you really don't take public transportation?"

"No, Mom. I'd have to travel with lumbar support and everything else I need for work. I don't mind the drive."

"How can you not? There's nothing to do but sit here. You can't even wave to people without them staring at you rudely." Her mom huffed.

Probably because she'd waved to every person they'd passed and not a one returned the gesture. "Mom, this isn't the South. People are in a hurry."

"Well so are we, but we're not moving."

"If you would've told me what hours you were looking to fly in, I could have advised you better."

"It's nine o'clock, dear. Shouldn't all these people be at work already?"

Shanée bit back a sigh. She'd tried to tell her mother about D.C. metro traffic, but it wasn't something easily understood until you'd been stuck on the streets for hours. It was one thing to say *hey it takes me two hours to make a thirty-minute drive every day for work* and it was something entirely different to sit in the car for two hours with everyone else driving out and about.

"Mom, just listen to the music. Breathe." *Please stop complaining!* They still had about an hour left until they arrived home.

"I'm sorry, dear. I'm not trying to stress you."

Shanée nodded in acknowledgment then flicked her blinker on to merge into the moving lane. The others had completely come to a standstill. There had to be an accident because traffic usually didn't stop this time of day.

A few minutes later, they bypassed a three-car pileup. *God, I pray they're okay. Please bring healing if needed and be with the first responders.* She gulped, hoping no one had an injury that would change the course of their life forever.

Then again, if she hadn't been hurt, would she have ever moved to D.C.? Met Gabe, who was actually pretty wonderful.

Even if she didn't want to saddle him with her baggage, it didn't stop her from admiring him from afar.

"How is working going?" Dad asked from his spot in the backseat. He'd offered the passenger spot to Mom, always the gentleman.

"It's going well. I like the people." Which she wouldn't have imagined possible.

But spending time with Gabe over the course of the month had allowed her to open up and rid herself of some bitterness. That in turn had helped her connect with people like Beth and Lorlaine, two nice women she would have ignored if Gabe hadn't offered a better perspective.

Why was she thinking about him so much? Was it because of the texts when she'd been waiting for her mom?

"I'm glad."

"Me too."

"Have you met anyone special, dear?" Mom asked.

Shanée slid a neutral mask on. "Everyone's special, Mom."

Her mom snorted. "Nice sidestep, but that's not going to work. You know exactly what I meant."

"Why would anyone want to date me?" She jolted, surprised by the truth and vulnerability of her question.

"Because you're beautiful. Kind. Smart. A *veteran*." Mom ticked off the list on her fingers.

"Nah, she's still too young to date," Dad quipped from the back.

Shanée laughed. "I'll always be too young to date, according to you."

"That's right. Don't forget it."

"I appreciate both of you, but no guy wants to date a woman with health problems."

"Maybe most men won't, but the right one won't care. He'll move heaven and earth to make you his."

She raised her eyebrows at Dad's pronouncement.

"Oh honey," Mom sighed. "That was so beautiful." She patted Shanée on the arm. "That's exactly why I married your father."

"Because he spouts off pretty words?"

"No, because he means them."

Shanée immediately thought of Gabe. How he wanted to be the person she talked to. How he had systematically inserted himself into her life so that he was all she thought about. He had become a trusted person in her life. His actions matched his words.

"But isn't it wrong to make a man live with me? I mean, I can't go rock climbing or anything adventurous."

Her dad snorted. "Not a lot of Black men go rock climbing anyway."

She laughed. "Dad. That's a stereotype. Black people like the outdoors."

He harrumphed.

"Hush. Let her talk, Walter."

"Anyway," Shanée continued. "What if he wants a lifestyle that can't accommodate my needs?"

"Then he's not the right one," her parents chorused.

She would have laughed if the conversation didn't feel so . . . scary.

"Are you thinking of someone in particular?" her mom asked softly.

"May-be," Shanée drew out.

"Has this particular someone given you any hints that he won't try and take your needs into consideration?"

Actually . . . Gabe was more than considerate, but that didn't

87

necessarily translate to a love connection. Maybe he was just nice. Though, that moment in the hallway of his home, she thought she'd seen desire in his eyes.

If she hadn't walked away, would he have kissed her? Did she *want* him to kiss her?

Yes! No. She bit her lip. *I don't know!*

"Honey?"

Her mom broke through her inane thoughts. "Sorry. Yes. He is extremely considerate."

"Then maybe you're too much in your head. Take a leap of faith."

"I couldn't leap even if I wanted to." She bit her lip. "Sorry, didn't mean that to come out so sarcastic." Since the church incident, Shanée had been trying to talk to God. Telling Him her doubts, her fears, and asking for Him to show His goodness.

"No problem. I want to hear all about this young man. Give me all the details."

"Spare me, please," Dad groused.

Shanée laughed. "Actually, he invited us to a Christmas party at his parents' house. Only his parents are on vacation, so they won't be there. He and his siblings are throwing a rebellion party."

Mom's chuckles floated through the air. "That's fantastic. I'm assuming his parents know."

"Yes."

"We'd love to attend. I've got to meet him."

"I knew I should have traveled with my guns," Dad grumbled.

"Dad!"

"Walter!" Mom said at the same time.

"What? Declaring guns is a hassle. But next time, I won't let that stop me."

"Yes, you will." Mom said.

Shanée just laughed, thankful for her parents and the humor they brought with them. She thought about Gabe. *Would he want a relationship with me, Lord? Am I worthy of something like that?*

Your suffering doesn't disqualify you from His love and goodness. He still has wonderful plans for you. He still has a purpose for you.

Her mind parroted Gabe's words. Perhaps she'd been looking at this all wrong. Everyone was broken in spirit but that didn't stop most people from searching for happiness. Shanée had been blessed by God's forgiveness and His grace was sufficient. Maybe she just needed to thank Him for grace and reach for the moments in life that made it all worthwhile.

Like Gabe.

She bit her lip. When she went to the party, she would tell him how she felt. She wanted more with him and could only hope he wanted the same thing.

Chapter Eleven

Throwing a party on Christmas Eve was the best idea the Lewis siblings had ever come up with. Gabe wasn't sure why none of them had done this before. Maybe his parents' vacation had been good for them after all. Allowed them to spread their wings and prove they'd still get together and celebrate the gift of Christ.

Granted, walking into his childhood home without Mom calling from the kitchen or Dad lingering in his office until dinner was strange. His parents would fly back tomorrow. They'd already arranged for a car to pick them up. All they'd asked was that Gabe and the rest of the crew prepare the meals tomorrow. Angel had volunteered for breakfast detail, mentioning that Bishop would help her out in the kitchen. Starr volunteered for desserts, and the rest of them were in charge of the main meal and the sides. Gabe figured he couldn't mess up yams, so he'd already snuck his mom's recipe from her binder. He'd return it before she'd miss the card.

But that was neither here nor there. He simply needed something else to think about as he waited for Shanée to show up with her parents.

He walked from the hallway to the living room where guests already congregated. Noel, dressed in a suit and smiling at a toothy woman who kept batting her false eyelashes, held a tray of appetizers. Gabe was half tempted to rescue Noel, but he was beginning to think his big brother needed a woman to pull his head out of work. He always claimed he was too busy to date, but even Noel needed a break from crunching numbers.

Deep down, Gabe wondered if Noel was simply afraid of a relationship. Numbers were easy to figure out, women not so much. *Hmm.* Something to discuss with his sisters. They probably already had an opinion. Maybe they'd even throw their hats into the matchmaking ring as well.

Gabe scanned the room, noting people from work, people from childhood, but no Shanée. Where was she?

"Relax, little brother. Your lady love will be here soon so you can stop moping about."

Gabe laid an arm across Eve's back and squeezed, then tickled her. She yelped and backed away.

"That's what you get for insinuating I would ever mope. Don't you know men *brood*?"

She rolled her eyes. "Nope. I smelled the mope a mile away. Why do you think I left my friends for your sorry self?"

"Ouch." He placed a hand on his chest. "Who knew shots would be fired from my own sister."

Eve grinned. She nudged him with her elbow. "I like Shanée."

"Do you?" He studied her eyes, all jokes pushed aside.

"Yes. She keeps you on your toes. But more importantly, I like who you are with her."

"Really?" He tried to keep the insecure tone from his voice, after all this was his older sister. At the same time, he wanted reassurance.

"Really. If she doesn't see how special you are, then I'll tell Dad to fire her."

He laughed. "Please don't. I'll get over it." He shrugged. "Maybe we'll remain friends." Just saying that soured his stomach.

"Trust God's timing."

He arched an eyebrow. "Wow, sounding spiritually wise there, Eve."

"I have my moments."

He looked at her. "You good? You haven't mentioned seeing anyone recently."

She gulped. "Recovering from the last one."

"Anyone I need to mess up?"

She shook her head, and his antennae went up. She was a little *too* adamant, which meant either the guy really hurt her and she didn't want to see him again, or he *hurt* her and Gabe needed to grab Noel and have a "talk" with the man.

"Who was it? Jeremy?" That was the name of her last boyfriend, right?

"No. You didn't meet him." She waved a hand in the air. "Besides, it doesn't matter. We're so over."

He stepped closer. "Did he hurt you, Eve?"

"Not physically. I'll get over the mental anguish."

He wasn't sure if anyone ever did, but he understood the sentiment.

"Besides, your lady love just walked in with her parents."

He straightened. "Do I look okay?"

Eve laughed. "You look perfect, Gabriel Angel."

"Ugh, sisters."

"You love me," she called as he walked away and headed straight for Shanée and her parents.

Lord, please don't let me mess this up. Please, please, please.

"Hey Shanée," he greeted, hating the nerves wobbling his words.

"Gabe." She smiled then gestured toward the woman standing next to her. "This is my mom. Mom, this is Gabe."

"Nice to meet you, Mrs. Mitchell," he offered his hand.

"It's a delight to meet you, Gabe. Shanée has told us so much about you."

That was a good thing, right? He glanced at her, loving the way her cheeks bloomed with color. Whether that was a blush or her makeup, he couldn't quite tell. But he wanted it to be the former, so he was going with that.

"Hopefully it was all good."

"Oh, you sound like a real sweetheart. She told us how much you've helped her."

Great. Did Shanée see him as a friend because he was *helpful*? Had he shot himself in the foot?

"Oh, my Dad." Shanée placed a hand on the big guy next to her. The one taller than Gabe's 5'10 height. He gulped. "Mr. Mitchell."

"Mmm."

O-kay. This was going swell. Gabe cleared his throat. "My brother and brother-in-law are going around with appetizers if you're hungry." He glanced at his watch. "And dinner will be served in about twenty minutes. Then we'll have dancing outside."

Bishop had rented a makeshift dance floor from the company that had delivered one for Gabe's birthday party. They found the perfect spot in the backyard, far away from Mom's prize garden. No way anyone wanted to be blamed if something went wrong.

"That sounds wonderful. Shall we go find some appetizers, dear?" Shanée's mother asked her husband.

Shanée's father eyed Gabe but nodded to his wife.

Gabe let out a breath as they left them standing in the foyer. "They seem nice."

"And not a little wacky?" Shanée asked.

He chuckled. "Aren't all parents?"

"Yes!" She stepped forward.

But Gabe stepped back and motioned for her to turn. She smiled shyly as she did a small three-sixty, her emerald-green dress flaring a little at the skirt. The material looked velvety and smooth and made him want to pull her into his arms. But he had to remember the order of things. He didn't want to declare his feelings until they were on the dance floor.

"You look beautiful."

"Thank you." She motioned to his suit. "You look great."

"I try."

She laughed. "I'm sure. It must have been so difficult to put on a suit and shave your face."

"You laugh but shaving your face can be torture." He ran a hand, feeling weird at the smooth texture left behind. "I kind of miss the beard."

"I like this." She trailed a hand down his cheek.

His breath hitched. "Then I like it if you like it." *Shut up! Abort mission.* But it was like his mouth had run away from him. "I have a question for you."

Shanée drew in a breath. She wanted to grab Gabe by the lapels and demand he admit he liked her as much as she liked him. But that would be slightly deranged and so unlike her. Not to mention the action might tweak her back. Instead, she calmly smiled up at him, hoping he'd see the invitation to declare any and all romantic feelings and put her out of her misery.

"What's that?" she asked.

"How long would you say we've been courting?"

"W-what?" She blinked. So not what she thought he was going to say. "We haven't . . . We aren't—" She shut her mouth, her cheeks feeling a few degrees away from a hot flash.

He flashed a dimpled grin her way.

Oh wow. They looked so appealing without a layer of hair covering the grooves. She placed her cold hands on her face. How had her wish for him to admit liking her jumped straight to courting? *Courting?* Who even used words like that?

She peered up at him. "We haven't dated, Gabe," she stated calmly despite her heart keeping up cadence with the Little Drummer Boy.

"I didn't say dating, I said *courting*." He took a step closer.

"People don't use that term. They date. But we haven't dated," she clamped her mouth shut, feeling flustered.

"There was that one time at Heaven when we made hot chocolate."

She gaped. "Wait a minute. That wasn't a date . . . *courting*," she said after he raised an eyebrow. "Your family was there."

"Pretty sure family is always around in a courtship."

Her mouth dropped. "Really? But . . ." She wanted alone time with him.

Though that could be dangerous if they didn't establish boundaries to keep them on the right path.

"Not at all. Courting couples need chaperones, don't you think?"

Shanée didn't know *what* to think. "So, you're saying we've been c-courting?" Why was she tripping over the words? Hadn't she wanted Gabe to declare some feelings?

"Exactly. Don't forget the tree farm excursion, church outing—"

"Was that your intention all along?" She peered into his warm eyes. "To court me?" She could feel her cheeks heating.

There was something about the word that held a deeper meaning than dating. She wanted to check her reflection and make sure she looked good enough for this moment. But her heart was racing, and she didn't want to miss a single thing he said.

"It wasn't at first," he stepped closer. "I wanted to be your friend, get to know you better. But somewhere along the line, my heart became invested." He trailed a finger down her arm. "And I knew I wanted to commit to something more than spending time with you. I wanted to take care of you *and* your heart."

"You did that." She thought of the carriage ride and how the only thing missing was being able to hold his hand. "I've had a lot of fun getting to know you."

"Music to my ears."

She offered a shy smile. "So, all the outings with your family, you're counting that in the courtship?"

He nodded, gently reaching for her hands. "And the lunch dates."

"But we were at work."

"No one said courtship only had to happen in off hours. And now I've met your parents as well."

Her stomach did a somersault. "What are you saying then?" she whispered.

He tucked her hair behind her ear. "I'm saying you're it for me. And I'm sorry that I got things backwards, but here goes—will you be my girlfriend?"

She couldn't stop the smile that spread across her face. "I would love to be your girlfriend." And there was a slight relief that he wasn't proposing. She wasn't sure where he had been leading when he first mentioned courting.

He placed his hands on her waist. "If I slide my hands around your back, will I hurt you?"

She stiffened, almost forgetting the question she *had* to ask. "About that. It doesn't bother you?"

"Your back? I think the pain bothers you a whole lot more than it bothers me."

"No." She shook her head. "That didn't come out right. I mean, it doesn't bother you that I'm broken? That I'm in pain all the time?"

"Shanée . . ." he breathed. "Of course it bothers me, but that's because I can't do anything to help you. It bothers me that you have to live with chronic pain. However, none of that makes me look at you as less than. We're all broken in different ways. It's God who puts us back together."

She sighed. It was so true. God had steadily stitched her hurting heart. He blessed her with a job she loved and a man . . . Her heart felt full. "I *like* you, Gabriel Lewis."

He gently placed his forehead against hers. "And I *like* you, Shanée Mitchell."

"Are you gonna kiss me now?"

"It would be my pleasure. Besides, why do you think I maneuvered you toward the door?"

She looked up and spotted mistletoe. "Smooth moves."

He took her chin in his gentle hands and laid a soft kiss on her lips. She sighed, letting him take the lead as her heart fluttered with happiness. When he pulled back, she snuggled closer, wrapping her arms around his back. When he placed his palms against hers, she let out a murmur of delight.

"I'm not hurting you?"

"No," she whispered. Not wanting to break the moment with any loud noises. She just wanted to rest in his arms and thank God for bringing her happiness in the midst of her trial.

Right now, she could see His goodness like the nose on her face. *Thank You so much.*

Epilogue
CHRISTMAS DAY

Shanée sat up slowly. Gabe had texted, warning her that he was about to blast a bullhorn to wake up everyone in the house. He didn't want to scare her and have her jumping out of the guest bed in the Lewis family home.

It had been surreal spending the night. Gabe had shared with her of the tradition of waking up as a family. Then he'd invited Shanée and her parents to join them. She'd borrowed a pair of pajamas from Starr. After they opened presents and had breakfast, Shanée would go home with her parents. Later tonight, they'd meet up to attend a candlelight service.

Shanée was excited for both, but more than that, she was excited to say Gabe was her boyfriend now. Thank goodness she'd brought his gift with her last night. It had been easy to sneak to her car in the middle of the night and place the wrapped box under the tree. She couldn't wait to see his face and whether or not he liked what she'd picked out.

She'd made the purchase after he'd mentioned flipping homes as a side business. He wasn't ready to quit Cornwall & Lewis, and she could admit his way was smarter than her suggestion of jumping all-in.

A bullhorn blasted in the air and shouts of "Merry Christmas" rang in the hall. She padded out of one of the guestrooms and laughed when Marvel ran by shouting, "Merry Christmas. Wake up!"

Gabe followed with the bullhorn. He only stopped blaring the thing when Noel opened a door and threw a pillow at his head. Shanée laughed but clammed up when Mr. and Mrs. Lewis walked out into the hall. When had they arrived? They both wore matching red silk pajamas.

"We leave you alone for two weeks and all sorts of shenanigans break out," Mrs. Lewis said.

"Angel made cinnamon rolls, Mom," Gabe replied sweetly.

"With icing?"

"And chai tea," he added.

"Mmm. I guess that's okay."

Just then Mrs. Lewis spotted Shanée wearing Starr's borrowed pajamas. Suddenly she felt self-conscious. Did she look okay? Was the older woman wondering what she was doing in the house?

Gabe turned around and motioned for her to come forward. Why was she so nervous? Her hand trembled as it slid into Gabe's. He tugged her gently forward, murmuring out the side of his mouth, "It's going to be okay."

"I hope so."

"Hey Mom, you remember Shanée, right?"

"Of course I do." His mom glanced at Gabe then studied Shanée. "Did you go to the party last night?"

"I did. You have a beautiful home."

"Imagine my shock, they didn't destroy the place."

"Whatever," Gabe mumbled.

"Watch it, Gabriel Angel."

"Yes, ma'am."

Shanée held back a snicker. She was so going to use his first and middle name. She just didn't know when.

"Now you want to tell me why you're introducing me to a woman I've already met?"

Gabe's hand tightened around hers. "Because she's important to me."

His mom's eyes filled with tears. Shanée held her breath.

"You . . . you two," she motioned between them.

Gabe nodded. "She's agreed to be my girlfriend. We're courting." He winked at Shanée, and she let out the breath.

"Oh baby, it's about time. I thought my boys would keep me from having grandchildren forever."

She wrapped Gabe in a hug, and he let go of Shanée's hand, which was a good thing since his mom started swaying back and forth.

"Mom, stop it. Angel and Starr already made you grandparents."

"But my baby boy hasn't."

"And Shanée isn't my fiancée. She only just yesterday agreed to be my girlfriend."

"That's because you didn't get down on one knee," Shanée quipped.

His head shot around, and his mouth dropped.

She laughed. "I'm going to go get a cinnamon roll." Because she was a chicken and truly wasn't ready for him to pop the big question. One thing at a time.

The rest of the family quickly filled the dining room with chatter and noises of appreciation at the cinnamon rolls. It was a little surreal seeing her parents there with the Lewis family, but Shanée loved it. She loved the slight chaos of so many people, but most of all, she loved the togetherness.

After breakfast, Mr. Lewis directed them to the living room to exchange presents. Shanée was surprised to get a gift from each sibling. Noel got her a calculator. Eve presented her with a cashmere scarf. Angel gave her a gift card to a massage therapist. Starr gave her a gift card to a shoe store that specialized in pretty shoes with orthopedic appeal.

The gifts were all so thoughtful that her heart felt like it would explode. Was this what it was like to count it all joy in the midst of trials? She'd never understood that before, but looking around at this family that had embraced her, her heart finally got it.

Gabe came to sit next to her, the gift she'd wrapped in his hands. "How'd you sneak this in here, huh?"

She just grinned.

"Should I open it?"

"Or let whatever's in there go to waste." She feigned nonchalance, shrugging a shoulder.

"Yeah, I'm not doing that." He shredded the wrapping paper then groaned when a plain brown box was revealed. Using brute strength, he punctured the taped box and opened the flaps. Then he pulled out an envelope. "What's in here?"

"Only one way to find out." She nudged him with her elbow. "Open it, Gabe."

"That's what I've been doing," he grumbled.

She kissed his cheek.

"If I whine some more, will you do that again?" he asked, voice low enough to elicit goosebumps on her arm.

"Behave," she whispered.

He opened the envelope and blinked. Blinked some more. Then turned to face her, a look of shock covering his features.

"Is that a thank you or . . ." Her voice trailed off. It was too extravagant, wasn't it?

"You bought me a house?"

"It's not how you make it sound." She licked her lips. "It's pretty derelict. Consider it an investment for your business. Restore it, sell it, and make sure to take before-and-after pics so future clients can be in awe." *Shut up, Mitchell.*

"How? How could you . . .? How could you even afford this?"

"I'm a disabled vet. I collect a paycheck from Uncle Sam as well as the one from Cornwall & Lewis." She shrugged. "It was just sitting in savings. I promise it wasn't a lot." Okay, so maybe she'd gone too far.

He slid his hands around the back of her head and gently pulled her close to him. She fell into the kiss, sensing the underlining gratitude.

"I can't believe you. How did I get so fortunate?" he whispered.

"I'm the blessed one," she murmured back.

"My turn." He pulled a box from underneath the tree and passed it to her.

She carefully unwrapped the box, choking back laughter as Gabe urged her to go faster. When she finally broke the top open, there was another box inside. She let her laughter loose. "I can't believe we both did that."

"Great minds," he tapped his temple.

She opened the second box and found another one inside, this one small enough to rest in the palm of her hand. Velvety smooth black box that most likely held jewelry. Her palm grew sweaty with the implications. "Gabe?"

"It's not what you think it is and it is what you think it is."

"What? Are you trying to confuse me?"

He chuckled and grabbed the box. "This one is a promise for something more to come." He snapped open the box and exposed a simple infinity ring. The rose gold band glistened. He pulled it out and took her right hand in his then slid the ring on her ring finger. "A promise that I'm in this for the long haul and one day will buy something pretty for the other hand."

Tears filled her eyes and she hugged him. "I love it."

"Merry Christmas, Shanée."

"Merry Christmas, Gabe."

Acknowledgments

I can't believe another book is said and done. I'm so thankful for the people who helped me along the way.

Andrea Boyd, Jaycee Weaver, and Sarah Monzon, thank you ladies for always helping me. Your critiques and friendship mean the world to me. Is it too early to say, "Merry Christmas!"

I also have a few special thank yous. To Jaycee Weaver for giving me the genius idea of Gabe and Angel's middle names. To my husband for giving me the idea for Shanée's injury. You're the best! To Mikal Dawn for giving me Shanée's first name!

I'd also like to thank you readers for continuously picking up my books to read. It means more than I could ever say. You're the reason I'm doing what I love, and I hope you enjoyed another Lewis sibling story.

To my husband and children, thanks for putting up with the constant Christmas music as I wrote this story. One day I'll actually write a Christmas story in season so you won't be confused as to why Kelly Clarkson and others are wishing us a Merry Christmas while it's hot outside. Love you!

About the Author

Toni Shiloh is a wife, mom, and Christian contemporary romance author. Once she understood the powerful saving grace thanks to the love of Christ, she was moved to honor her Savior. She writes to bring Him glory and to learn more about His goodness.

She spends her days hanging out with her husband and their two boys. She is a member of the American Christian Fiction Writers (ACFW) and their Virginia Chapter.

You can find her on her website at http://tonishiloh.com. Sign up for her newsletter at http://eepurl.com/gcMfqT.

More Books by Toni Shiloh

Standalone novel

An Unlikely Proposal

Series

Maple Run Series

Buying Love

Finding Love

Enduring Love

Risking Love

Freedom Lake Series

Returning Home

Grace Restored

Finally Accepted

Faith & Fortune Series

The Trouble With Love

The Truth About Fame

The Price of Dreams

Novellas

A Proxy Wedding

A Sidelined Christmas

Deck the Shelves

Once Upon a Christmas

Something Borrowed

I'll Be Home

All I Want

Made in the USA
Monee, IL
06 January 2022